A Star in Winter

OTHER BOOKS AND BOOKS ON CASSETTE
BY ANITA STANSFIELD:

First Love and Forever

First Love, Second Chances

Now and Forever

By Love and Grace

A Promise of Forever

Return to Love

To Love Again

When Forever Comes

For Love Alone

Home for Christmas

A Christmas Melody

The Gable Faces East

Gables Against the Sky

The Three Gifts of Christmas

Towers of Brierley

TALK ON CASSETTE

Find Your Gifts, Follow Your Dreams

A Star in Winter

a novel

ANITA
STANSFIELD

Covenant Communications, Inc.

Covenant

Published by Covenant Communications, Inc.
American Fork, Utah

Printed in the United States of America
First Printing: October 2000

07 06 05 04 03 02 01 00   10 9 8 7 6 5 4 3 2 1

ISBN 1-57734-682-3

Library of Congress Cataloging-in-Publication Data

Stansfield, Anita, 1961-
    A star in winter / Anita Stansfield.
        p. cm.
    ISBN 1-57734-682-3
    1. Divorced fathers--Fiction. 2. Fathers and sons--Fiction. 3. Women teachers--Fiction.
I. Title.

PS3569.T33354 S72 2000
813'.54--dc21   00-043056

For Cindy, Kim, Dianne, LaRene, & Deanna

Happy Birthday!

Prologue

Provo, Utah

Shayne Brynner hung up the telephone and let out a deep sigh. He pressed both hands into his hair and felt almost faint from the reality that lay before him. The news that his home had sold was an answer to many prayers. Now he would be able to pay off their debts in full, and he could afford to start putting money away to start over. He could stop having nightmares of financial ruin. The relief was indescribable. Then why did he have this smoldering knot in the pit of his stomach, and this dizzying ache between his eyes? Why did he have to believe in his heart that the path to solving one set of problems was the avenue to seeing other aspects of his life destroyed? Of course, he'd fasted and prayed about his decision to sell the house, and he knew beyond any doubt that it was the right thing to do. It had been his only choice in the face of bankruptcy. But even then he had known Margie would balk at the idea—and she had. Her angry words had been catapulting relentlessly through his mind ever since. *"I don't know how you could just sell the house right out from under me. How can you be so cruel and insensitive?"*

Shayne had carefully pointed out, as he had dozens of times before, that this drastic measure wouldn't have become necessary if she had curbed her superfluous spending. As usual, Margie had ignored him in order to persist with her criticism of his incompetence as a husband and father. In the weeks since, Shayne had studied it out in his mind so many times that a pounding headache was becoming his constant companion. He'd spent long, sleepless nights staring toward the ceiling, praying for strength and guidance, desperately wanting to see the situation realistically. *Was* he being cruel and insensitive? Was there something wrong with *him?* He certainly wasn't perfect, and he'd spent the nine years of his marriage working very hard to search out his weaknesses and correct them. Margie had certainly been eager to help point them out and guide him continually in his efforts. But now he was left with a stack of credit card receipts with her signature on them, along with an unsettling feeling that this was the beginning of the end. No, he rationalized, unable to face the possibility. Surely they could get over this hurdle together. As hard as it was, perhaps this was the beginning of some necessary—and positive—changes.

Deep in his heart, he believed he had done everything he could to make his marriage work. Surely his efforts had to pay off eventually. Still, that didn't change the harsh reality of what he now had to face. In the weeks since the realtor's sign had been posted in the front yard, Margie had been relatively quiet and spent most of her time in the bedroom recliner, with the remote control to the television close at hand. The children had started school and seemed to be doing well— all things considered. They were used to their mother doing very little with or for them, and Shayne was quite accustomed to coming home from work to put in a load of laundry and throw together something for the family to eat. Margie's "heart condition" was always the reason for her passive role as a mother and homemaker. But Shayne knew from at least five professional opinions that Margie's condition was not a concern beyond the need to avoid strenuous athletic activity. She'd been told dozens of times that she could live a normal and productive life, and reasonable exercise was a good thing. But the only exercise Margie ever got was walking through the mall with her friends, always returning with an armload of packages. When several fervent pleas to curb her spending had failed, Shayne had finally cut up the credit cards and lived with a silently angry woman for weeks. His decision to sell the house had been received in a similar fashion, but it had settled more quickly. From what little Margie had said to him, he figured that she had convinced herself the house wouldn't sell, or that somehow he would back down and follow her suggestion to file for bankruptcy rather than upset their comfort zone and move temporarily into an apartment. But now the house had sold, and he wondered why he felt almost guilty for praying so hard that it would. Shayne was now faced with the horrid task of telling his wife that they would soon be moving. To say she wouldn't take it well seemed a gross understatement. He honestly had no idea what to expect. He'd prayed and prayed that her heart would soften, that she would see that no matter where they were or how much money they had, they could be a family. They just had to be! Any other possibility was unthinkable.

Chapter 1

Six Weeks Later

Helen Starkey sat contemplatively at her desk, discreetly observing the little flock of third-graders in her care. It was a common practice for her to use their reading time each day for her own silent appraisal. One by one she watched each child while they were unaware, mentally going through a checklist of behavior, attitude, and academic performance. If she was uncertain on any matter, she quickly checked her records of assignments and scores, and made subsequent notes. But the evidence of a child's self-worth was far more important to Helen than any list of numbers and grades. And she felt gratified at the moment to assess her little flock and feel relatively good about each individual. Except one.

Scotty Brynner. Oh, there were always little problems here and there with a number of the children. But Scotty had started out the school year as a typical eight-year-old boy: relatively bright, slightly mischievous, and full of energy. He was well dressed, clean, and apparently healthy. A few weeks into the school year she had begun to notice the changes, and they'd become steadily worse. Now, with Halloween approaching, it suddenly struck her that his social and academic decline had been sure and steady. She couldn't count the times she'd left messages on the family answering machine, not to mention the notes she had sent home in sealed envelopes for Scotty's parents. She'd never gotten any response on either count.

Helen knew that Scotty lived in a two-parent home. She had also gleaned from his delightful chatter near the beginning of the year that his family was active in the Church, and he'd been recently baptized. But there was obviously a missing puzzle piece here, and it was becoming increasingly difficult to know what to do for him. She had attempted to talk to Scotty a number of times, but he was evasive and withdrawn.

The bell's ringing startled Helen from her thoughts, and the quiet room became a bustle of activity and young voices excitedly preparing for lunch. Once the children were settled in the cafeteria, Helen took her insulated lunch bag to the teachers' lounge and dug out her Rubbermaid bowl of pasta salad, along with some cheese and crackers, and a little bottle of V-8 Juice. She'd barely opened her juice when Carla came in to join her.

"Hey there, cutey," she said, sitting across the table from Helen. "How's the chewing gum patrol?"

"No gum today," Helen replied. "How's the rubber band patrol?"

"Confiscated six of them," Carla said as if they were discussing national security, then they both laughed. Carla took closer notice of what Helen was eating and whined comically, "Hey, no fair. Your lunch looks better than mine. I'll trade you half a tuna on whole wheat for some of that salad."

"I'm one step ahead of you," Helen said, pulling out another bowl and an extra plastic fork.

"Way cool," Carla said. "You're a sweetie, as always."

"I just know you," Helen said, perusing a *Family Circle* magazine that had been left by another teacher. "You always like my food better. Besides, nobody else eats my cooking. You might as well."

"I *love* your cooking," Carla said with her mouth full.

Helen smiled and continued to idly flip pages while she ate, and Carla rambled in her typical way about the antics of her three children, ages seven to twelve. Helen loved hearing about them, as long as she ignored the subtle ache that rose inside her each time she bothered to compare her life to Carla's. The two of them had been teaching third grade across the hall from each other for over five years. There was no doubt that Carla was Helen's best friend. They had so much in common that they could almost read each other's minds. There was only a four months' difference in their ages. They were both returned missionaries, currently teaching Primary, and they continually exchanged recipes and teaching ideas. But while Carla had a sweet husband and three adorable children at home, Helen had a cat named Twinkle.

Lunch was over too quickly. Helen and Carla stood side by side just outside the large double doors that led in from the playground. They each held up a brightly painted cardboard cutout, glued to a flat ruler, so the children could easily find the teacher where they needed to line up. Helen's was a fluorescent yellow star with a happy face on it. Carla's was a white cow with black spots, wearing a silly grin. The cow represented Carla's artistic abilities. She was gifted—at least when it came to drawing cows. She could draw her cartoonish bovines with any expression you could think of. And her classroom was full of cows. Cow knickknacks. A cow calendar. Spotted cow fabric covering the piano bench and framing the bulletin board. Carla had a cow apron that she wore for story time. Cow earrings and cow necklaces. She had cow sweatshirts and wrote letters on cow stationery. And Helen knew what Carla's students did not: that her car had cow seat covers and her kitchen at home had similar decor, right down to the cow salt and pepper shakers. Of course, Helen teased her about it. But then, Carla teased Helen right back.

Helen's classroom was filled equivalently with stars. It had initially started as a school joke. During her first few months of teaching, many of the children got her name wrong. The faculty picked up on it and started giving her prank gifts with stars on them. And it stuck.

"At least I didn't decorate my kitchen with stars," Helen often said to Carla.

"Oh, no," Carla would retort. "You just named your cat Twinkle."

Helen liked being *Miss Star.* At least the star part. The *Miss* was something she still had a problem with. She had often studied herself in the mirror, and had to admit that she wasn't half bad to look at. Her long, brown curly hair was flattering. Her features were average, but more than pleasant. She couldn't deny that she'd thickened up with age, but she knew how to dress to her best advantage. And she knew countless women her age who were happily married with no less extra weight on them—Carla being one of them. In high school, Helen had dated as much as any other girl. In college it had been the same. She'd even had a few marriage proposals, and she'd seriously considered accepting more than one of them. But in her heart she had known that it wasn't right. Eventually, when there simply weren't any available men her age worth even sharing a movie with, she had stopped dating altogether. She wasn't bitter by any means. She wasn't even what she could call unhappy. She loved her job. She loved her home. She loved to cook. And she loved her cat. But there was an emptiness in Helen that she was beginning to believe would be with her for the rest of her life. She'd done her best to accept it and make the most of all she'd been blessed with, but still . . . there was an emptiness.

Helen and Carla chatted comfortably until all the children were lined up and accounted for, then they were led inside like a bunch of baby ducks following their mothers out of the pond. The teachers shared a typical histrionic parting wave that made the children laugh, then they went into their separate rooms with their ducklings right behind.

Through the afternoon, while the children made skeletons from cutting up white paper plates, Helen kept an especially close eye on little Scotty Brynner, and her concern deepened. She made up her mind that she was going to pay a visit to his parents that evening. One way or another, she was going to find out what the problem was and get to the bottom of it. She'd learned long ago not to prejudge any situation, but she couldn't help wondering why parents wouldn't respond to a teacher's concerns and offer support with the education of their children.

After school let out for the day, Helen stayed a short while to be certain everything was in order for tomorrow. Then she drove the short distance to her home. Just last year she had purchased the house, using every bit of savings she had and borrowing everything she could get her hands on. It was bigger than what she needed, but she had felt good about it, knowing beyond any doubt that it was the right house for her. In the brief time she'd lived here she had come to feel very much at home in the ward and the neighborhood, and she could well imagine growing old here—with a cat.

"Hello, Twinkle," she said just inside the back door as the cat rubbed her leg and left a spattering of white hair on her black stocking.

While the cat clung to her legs and purred, Helen got the mail, removed her shoes, and poured herself a tall glass of grape juice on ice. She relaxed for a while, then heated up some of the lasagne she'd made the night before.

Feeling especially tired, she decided to wait until tomorrow to visit the Brynner family. But Scotty wasn't at school the following day. She called the number on her lunch break, but only the machine answered. And she spent the afternoon with an increasing uneasiness that sent her straight to the Brynner home as soon as school was over and her work was done.

Pulling up in front of a nice split-level home, Helen double checked the address she had copied down from her school records. A woman in her early thirties answered the door, and Helen put on a smile. "Mrs. Brynner?" she said.

"Uh . . . no. The Brynners moved just a couple of weeks ago."

Helen was momentarily stunned. "Oh. Well, I'm sorry. Do you know where, by chance?"

"I'm afraid not," the woman smiled, and Helen returned to her car to contemplate her next move. She quickly dialed the school office on her cell phone, hoping the secretary hadn't left early today. She felt her luck improving when she had the new address within minutes.

The apartment was easy to find, only a couple of blocks from the school. She knocked at the door, glancing around briefly as she wondered what would require a move from a nice home to an apartment that seemed old and a little run-down. Hearing a television, she knocked a second time, then heard a familiar young voice call, "Who is it?"

"It's Miss Star," she called back. "Is that you, Scotty?"

Following a long moment of silence, the door came open little more than a crack.

"Hi, Scotty," she said, putting on her bright school-teaching face. "I missed you in school today and thought I would bring you your work."

Scotty said nothing.

"Is your mother at home?" Helen asked.

Scotty said nothing. He wouldn't look at her.

"Is your father at home?" Still nothing. "Are you with a baby-sitter, or—"

"The baby-sitter didn't come," he said, as if she'd come upon a question he could answer without breaking some kind of rule.

"Are you alone then?" she asked gently. He glanced at her hesitantly. "Listen, Scotty, I know you're not supposed to answer such questions when you talk to strangers. But I'm your teacher, and I care very much about you. I just need to talk to your father or your mother. Could you tell me when I could find them home?"

Scotty shook his head.

"Are you alone?" she repeated.

"Tamara's here."

"Is that your sister?" Helen asked, and he nodded. "You're alone with your sister?" she asked to clarify.

"The baby-sitter didn't come," he repeated. Then, with no warning, big tears welled in his eyes.

Helen went to her knees to meet him at eye level. "Scotty, what is it? What's wrong?" He only sniffled and she added, "I want to help you, Scotty." He seemed wary, and Helen uttered a silent prayer, hoping to find a way to let him know that she had his best interests at heart. She felt the need to help him, and an equal need to get some information concerning a number of obvious difficulties. A moment later she said, "Do you remember when you were baptized, Scotty, and you were given the gift of the Holy Ghost?" He nodded, and his eyes were a little brighter. "One of the things that gift can do for you is to let you know in your heart if something is right or not. I would like to come in and stay with you until your parents come home, and I could help you with your schoolwork. But if you don't feel good about that, then you just have to say so and I'll come back later."

Scotty looked thoughtful for a long moment, then he opened the door wide. Helen stepped inside and he closed it loudly. The little front room and adjacent dining area were relatively tidy except for a few scattered coloring books and toys, and a few dirty dishes on the table. But it felt dark and close with all of the curtains tightly shutting out the afternoon sun. *Wishbone* played on the little television, and Tamara was curled up on the couch, absorbed in it. She glanced up at the closing of the door and gave a hint of a smile. "Hi, Miss Star," she said, as if seeing her here was the most natural thing in the world.

"Hello, Tamara," she said, recognizing her now as a child she often passed in the school halls. "How was school today?"

"Oh, I didn't go," she answered as if they were peers. "But I like school. Mrs. Bills is cool." *First grade,* Helen thought as Tamara continued. "I stayed home to be with Scotty 'cause he had a stomachache and he was scared. He stayed home with me when I was scared, so I told him I would stay home with him. He's feeling better now, though. Our baby-sitter was supposed to come after school but she didn't. That's okay, though, 'cause me and Scotty are together. Dad should be home about six, if you want to talk to him."

"Thank you," Helen said with a little laugh. At least Tamara talked more freely than her brother. That could definitely help in getting information.

While Tamara turned her attention back to the television, Helen asked Scotty, "Would you like me to go over your schoolwork with you?"

"Okay," he said, not seeming too reluctant.

They sat together at the table in the little dining area, and Helen asked, "Does your stomach still hurt?"

"No," he said, "it's better now."

This made Helen wonder if he'd had one of those *I don't want to go school* illnesses. Together they went over the work he had missed, and she was grateful for the opportunity to spend this one-on-one time with him. She was pleasantly surprised to realize that he was still as quick and sharp as he'd ever been in his math concepts and spelling. Eliminating that as a problem, she wondered why he hadn't been turning in his homework, and why his test scores had been so poor. She wondered if it might be the same reason the family had moved, and the children were being left alone. She felt a temptation to be angry with these parents, but she reminded herself of the fact that she had no idea what was taking place here, and she had no right to make judgments.

When Tamara's favorite PBS programs ended at five o'clock, she wandered into the little kitchen and stood staring into an open refrigerator.

"Are you hungry?" Helen asked, and both children responded with firm nods.

"Let's see what we can find, shall we?" she asked, certain she could fix them some kind of a snack.

She found cheese and contemplated grilled sandwiches, but there was only one slice of bread. She cut some of the cheese into little cubes and stuck toothpicks in them, but they were quickly gone. Helen glanced at the dirty dishes in the sink and the contents of the garbage can. Macaroni and cheese, canned soup, peanut butter sandwiches, cold cereal. It didn't take a detective to see that this family hadn't been eating home cooking.

"Do you think it would be all right if I cooked some supper for you?" she asked, and again the children nodded eagerly.

"Can we help?" Tamara asked, scooting a chair close to the counter, which she promptly stood on.

"Well, I don't want to do it alone," Helen said. She quickly perused the cupboards and fridge, contemplating the recipes filed in her head for a simple casserole. "Have you ever eaten hamburger pie?" she asked.

"No," they both said together. "Is it good?" Tamara questioned.

"I think so. Would you be willing to try it?"

They both agreed, and together they peeled potatoes and put them on to cook. A small package of ground beef from the freezer was quickly thawed in the microwave, then browned on the stove with some simple seasonings. Tomato sauce was added to the hamburger mixture, and then a can of green beans.

"You put *beans* in there?" Scotty declared with disgust.

"I'll make you a deal," Helen said. "If you'll close your eyes and eat three big bites, I'll bet you some cookies that you'll like it."

"What do you mean . . . cookies?" he asked skeptically.

"If you like it, I'll bring some cookies over tomorrow for you and your mom and dad."

"Mom won't be here," Tamara said.

"Where is your mother?" Helen asked, hoping this would be some of the information she was looking for.

"She went to live with Grandma," Tamara said. "She's sick, and Grandma's taking care of her."

"I see," Helen said while she mashed the potatoes and spread them over the hamburger mixture in an oblong pan. The children wrinkled their noses but made no comment. Helen let the children sprinkle cheese over the top while she tried to read between the lines of everything she'd observed with this little family today.

What illness did Mrs. Brynner suffer from? And how long had she been staying with "Grandma"? Did the mother's poor health have anything to do with the family's moving from their home? Had financial problems been a factor? She mentally filed through the possible diseases Mrs. Brynner might have, and her heart ached at the situation. It certainly put some perspective on Scotty's change in behavior and performance in school. But she wondered what could be done.

While the casserole was in the oven, they worked together to wash up the dirty dishes and wipe off the table and counters. As they sat down to eat, with a place set for their father, Helen hoped Mr. Brynner wouldn't come home and get angry with her for having invaded his home. They said a blessing, then the children took Helen's challenge literally. They closed their eyes and each bravely took a big bite of hamburger pie. Then they both laughed and admitted it was yummy.

"You see," Helen said, "some things taste better than they look."

While they shared their little meal, Helen was glad she'd gained some perspective before coming face to face with Mr. Brynner. Putting the pieces together now, she could well imagine how stressed and overwhelmed he must feel with his wife gone and suffering from illness, being left to care for his children on his own, and having financial problems to boot. While the children ate an exorbitant amount, Helen's mind wandered through the possibilities. Then she heard the key turning in the door and suddenly felt very nervous. She had no idea how this man was going to respond to finding her here, and she quickly gathered up her dirty dishes and carried them to the sink.

"Daddy! Daddy!" Tamara said, running from the table.

Helen heard a deep laugh of genuine delight followed by a vibrant, "How's my little Snickerdoodle today?"

"I'm fine, but Scotty had a stomachache so we didn't go to school."

A deep sigh followed the confession. "I thought I told you to call me if you stayed home," he said gently. "I don't like having you here all alone."

"We were okay," Tamara said in the same grown-up tone she had used with Helen. "I took good care of Scotty, and we could have called you if we needed you. But you said you need to be at work. We didn't answer the phone, just like you said. And we didn't answer the door except when Miss Star came, and Scotty asked who it was before he opened it. And since Courtney didn't come and—"

"Courtney didn't come *again?*" he asked, obviously irritated.

"No, but that's okay, 'cause Miss Star came, and she helped Scotty with his homework, and we cooked pie with green beans in it, and—"

"Wait a minute. Wait a minute. Who are you talking about?"

Helen forced herself to appear before the child got into trouble. At least Tamara had alleviated the need for much of the necessary explanation. "Uh . . . that would be me," Helen said, coming around the corner from the kitchen.

The man squatting beside Tamara suddenly sprang to his feet, obviously startled at finding a stranger in his home. Hoping he wouldn't be angry with her, she hurried to explain. "Uh . . . I'm Scotty's schoolteacher."

"Miss Star," Scotty said quickly, and she noticed him smiling. It was good to see him smile.

Helen chuckled tensely. "It's Miss Starkey, actually, but the children call me Miss Star. Anyway, I came to check on Scotty, and when I realized they were alone, I stayed and . . . well, I hope you won't be upset with the children . . . or me . . . or . . ."

She was trying to find an end to her stammering when he said, "You must forgive me for not returning your calls."

She expected him to give some kind of explanation, but he didn't. She felt some relief to see that he seemed as embarrassed as she felt. During a brief moment of silence, she took in his appearance. He obviously worked outdoors by the way he was dressed—construction, perhaps. He was a little above average height, with dark wavy hair and a face so boyish that he almost seemed like a larger replica of his son. She guessed him to be a little younger than herself; *apparently healthy, seems well adjusted, perhaps a bit distracted.* Startled by her train of thought, Helen told herself she needed to get out more. She was beginning to assess everyone she met as if they were a new student.

Realizing that it was her turn to say something, Helen muttered quickly, "There's no need to apologize, Mr. Brynner. It's evident that you've been very busy."

This seemed to increase his embarrassment as he glanced down and said, "I admit to being overwhelmed, Miss Star . . . uh, Starkey. But that's no excuse to neglect my children's needs. I really meant to get to parent-teacher conference, but . . . well, I don't remember exactly why I didn't make it. Perhaps we could schedule some time and see what needs to be done."

"That would be great," she said. "I was hoping for that very thing."

Scotty broke the next stretch of silence with the announcement, "Miss Star cooked supper. Come and eat, Daddy. It's good, even though it has green beans in it. And since we liked it, she's going to bring us cookies tomorrow."

Helen chuckled and said to Scotty, "That's right. Now, if you're finished, why don't you rinse off your dishes." She then said to Mr. Brynner, "I hope you don't mind. The children were hungry and I just thought I'd pull a little something together while I was waiting."

"Mind? No, of course not. I don't know how to thank you. I've had a real challenge with finding a sitter I can depend on. I appreciate your help."

"Glad to do it, really." Helen reached for her purse. "Why don't you wash up and eat while it's still warm. I think there's enough to heat up for tomorrow and . . . well, perhaps we could talk sometime soon about Scotty, and—"

"How about right now?" he asked, then looked briefly alarmed. "Unless you're in a hurry, of course."

"No, I'm not, actually. Now would be fine, as long as I'm here."

He hurried to wash up, then asked the children to go in the other room and play for a little while so he and Scotty's teacher could talk privately.

"Am I in trouble?" Scotty asked.

"No, Scooter," his father said. "I think *I'm* in trouble

for not seeing that you stayed on top of your assignments. We'll work on it together, but first I need to talk
with Miss Starkey."

The children hurried away, and Mr. Brynner sat at
the table to eat.

"Forgive me," Helen said, unable to go on without
clearing the air, "but I have to admit that I'm really glad
you weren't angry with me. I know it was pretty
presumptuous of me to come into your house and . . .
use your kitchen and . . . Anyway, I was just acting on
my feelings, but you would have been justified in being
upset with me, and . . . well, thank you for *not* being
upset with me."

Mr. Brynner chuckled softly. "It's all right, Miss
Starkey. I have to admit, there are some people I probably would have been upset with for doing the same
thing. But it's obvious you have a good heart, and you
were only concerned for the children's best interests."

"How do you know that?" Helen asked, not
completely serious. Their eyes met for a moment, and
she wondered if the same subtle feelings that had
prompted her to be here now were easing his concerns.

"I just know," he said, and proceeded to eat.

Smiling at an occasional enthusiastic compliment on
her cooking, Helen quietly explained her observations
and concerns. She expected, or at least hoped, for a
more specific explanation regarding their circumstances.
But he simply said, "We've all had some tough adjustments lately, and Scotty seems to accept change less
readily than Tamara. I'm certain that when his mother
comes back, things will settle down for him. But in the
meantime, I'll do my best to help him."

Helen made some simple suggestions that would help him keep track of Scotty's homework without taking too much time out of his already busy schedule. She promised to check back, and he promised to return her calls.

When the little meeting was apparently finished, Helen stood to go, and he rose to walk her to the door. As he reached for the knob, Helen knew she couldn't leave without making the offer that had been catapulting through her head for the last several minutes.

"Listen," she said, turning back to face him, "if you're having trouble finding someone to stay with the children after school, maybe I could help. I only need to work a short while after class is finished. They could wait in my classroom. There's plenty to keep them busy. Then I could bring them home and stay with them until you get here." Sensing he would protest, she hurried to explain, "There's no one who will miss me except my cat, and she's spoiled as it is. I can sit here and grade papers as easily as I can at home. I'd really love to help out. And perhaps I could help Scotty get caught up, as well."

Helen met his eyes briefly, and there was no imagining the barely detectable glisten of tears she saw there. She glanced away so as not to embarrass him. He cleared his throat quietly and said, "I don't know what to say. You can't imagine how much worry that would alleviate."

"I'm glad to do it," she said, and left as soon as she'd said good-bye to the children.

Helen drove the short distance to her home feeling a gratification that was delightfully unfamiliar. Her ordinary act of cooking a meal had been truly needed and appreciated. The opportunity to share her time and abilities in a simple way that made a difference meant more to her than she could describe. Of course, she did that every day; teaching was a part of her, and she knew she was making a difference in these children's lives. But her opportunity to help the Brynner family now added something to her life that had been missing. It was as simple as that.

Helen pulled into her garage and pushed the button for the automatic door to close behind her. She smiled to herself as she went into the house, looking forward to tomorrow afternoon. Twinkle met her at the door, overflowing with anxious meowing, as if to say, *How dare you stay out late without my permission! You've been neglecting me, and you should be ashamed of yourself.* But a few extra scratches under the chin soon had Twinkle purring. And a rare treat of canned cat food made up for the negligence.

Remembering her promise, Helen hurried to mix up a batch of oatmeal-chocolate chip cookies and put the dough in the fridge in a Zip-Loc bag. She went to bed imagining baking cookies with Tamara and Scotty, and realized she felt happier than she had in a long, long time. Not that her life wasn't happy. She simply felt more content than usual tonight.

HAMBURGER PIE

Brown 1 lb. ground beef and add the following to taste:

> *Salt and pepper*
> *Minced onion*
> *Garlic powder*
> *Dried parsley*
> *Worcestershire sauce*

Add: *One can of green beans, drained*
Two 8-oz. cans of tomato sauce

Spread in casserole dish and spread hot mashed potatoes on top.
Sprinkle with shredded cheese and put in 350° oven until cheese is melted.

Close your eyes and take three bites!

Chapter 2

Helen found her normally enjoyable day even more so as she anticipated doing something worthwhile after school. With her bag of cookie dough concealed in a brown paper sack in the faculty lounge fridge, she counted down the hours until school was out.

"So, you think she's got cancer or something?" Carla asked her over lunch.

"I don't know. But it sounds like something pretty serious. Obviously the family has made a lot of sacrifices because of her illness, whatever it is."

"Wow," Carla said, then she took a bite of the turkey pita sandwich with sprouts that Helen had given her. "Sure makes me appreciate what I've got—good health, for one thing."

"I had the same thought," Helen agreed.

"Then I guess your afternoons are going to be pretty busy for a while."

"Yes, they are," Helen said with a little laugh.

"I take it you like that idea."

"Very much, actually."

"So this Mr. Brynner . . . what's he like?"

"I don't know. Just a guy. Seems like a good dad from

what little I observed. He was polite and gracious. I was really afraid he'd get angry or defensive to find me invading his kitchen."

"Some guys probably would have been. I've seen more than a few daddies who would be, given the same circumstances."

"Yeah, me too," Helen said.

Carla chuckled. "He was probably afraid you'd turn him in to Social Services."

"Oh, I never thought of that. Do you really think he would believe that I . . ."

"Well, it's evident he's not willfully neglecting his children. He's simply adjusting. But I know some teachers . . ." She leaned closer and whispered dramatically, "We won't mention any names . . . who would have only looked at the technicality that his kids had been alone all day and would have blown the whistle."

"Well, I'm glad it was me who was there, and not . . . well . . . we won't mention any names." They both laughed, with no need to discuss a particular faculty member who was a self-appointed Social Services patrol. The little good she had done in getting government help for families where it was needed had been far outweighed by the problems she had caused with her hasty judgments and sticking her nose where it didn't belong.

"I'm glad it was you, too," Carla added. "Let me know how it goes."

Through the afternoon, Helen noticed that Scotty seemed a little more like himself. He was still somewhat withdrawn from the other children, but he seemed more focused on his work; and occasionally, when she caught his eye, he gave her a subtle smile. She wondered if he was anticipating their being together this afternoon, just as she was.

When school was out, Tamara appeared in Helen's room just a few minutes after the other children left. "Hi, Miss Star," she said, setting her backpack on the desk next to where Scotty was still sitting.

"How are you today, Tamara?"

"I'm fine. How are you?" she asked and Helen chuckled softly at Tamara's six-going-on-twenty-one disposition.

"I'm doing great. You know, I was thinking that if the two of you get your homework and reading done while I finish up my work, then you can help me bake cookies when we get home."

They both responded with enthusiasm and dug into their worksheets. Occasionally they asked her for a little help, and Tamara sat beside Helen so she could help her sound out the new words in her simple reader.

Helen finished up in her classroom just as the janitor was coming in to empty wastebaskets and vacuum the carpet. He teased the children for a minute and then they were off, stopping only to get the cookie dough out of the faculty room fridge. "I had to put it in a brown paper bag," she said to the children on their way to the parking lot, "or the other teachers would have been snitching cookie dough and we wouldn't have had any left."

The children giggled, apparently finding the idea terribly amusing.

Upon arriving at the apartment, Scotty opened the door with a key pinned inside his pocket with a safety pin. Things were relatively tidy, and the few dirty dishes that had been left the previous evening had been washed. She also noticed that they had gone grocery shopping. There was more milk and juice, and a fresh loaf of bread, as well as cereal and canned goods in the cupboard.

They baked cookies together, ate some while they were still warm, and put the rest into a large Rubbermaid bowl to keep them moist. The children watched *Arthur* on PBS while Helen checked school papers. With supper time at hand, she searched for the leftover hamburger pie to heat up, and found that it was gone except for a tiny portion. When she asked the children about it, Scotty simply said, "Dad ate some for breakfast."

Helen fixed grilled cheese sandwiches and cut them into little triangles to eat with their bowls of chicken noodle soup, and added some canned pears to the menu. She made a mental note to ask Mr. Brynner if he would mind having her help with some grocery shopping. A little variety seemed to be in order.

Mr. Brynner arrived soon after they had eaten. While he greeted his children and asked about their day, she reheated the soup and hurried to make him a fresh grilled-cheese sandwich.

"Hello, Miss Starkey," he said, startling her as she set his sandwich on a plate.

"Oh, hello," she replied with a smile. "Good day?"

"It was much better, knowing that my children were being cared for."

"I'm glad," she said. "I've fixed a sandwich for you. The children have done their homework."

"Thank you," he said, seeming slightly embarrassed. He cleared his throat and added, "Listen, I was thinking that I really should pay you for your time. I know it's—"

"Heavens, no," she insisted. "I wouldn't hear of it. I'm rather enjoying myself, actually."

"But surely you could use some extra money to—"

"No, I really don't need it. Please, just let me do this." She thought of how she'd sunk everything she had into getting her home. She was making ends meet just fine, but she wouldn't be able to afford to go home for Christmas this year. Still, she knew that accepting his money under the circumstances would take some of the joy out of what she was doing. Besides, she felt certain that he couldn't afford it.

"Are you sure?" he asked. "Because the last thing I want to do is take unfair advantage of you when you've been so kind."

"I'm sure," she said. "Now, why don't you eat before it gets cold, and I'll be on my way."

"Thank you again," he said, walking her to the door.

"You're very welcome, and . . . oh," she turned back, "I was thinking . . . how would you feel about my doing some grocery shopping for you? I'm pretty good at shopping on a budget, and I could get some things to cook for suppers and . . . well, you must be getting tired of macaroni and cheese. Aren't you?"

Mr. Brynner laughed comfortably. "I certainly am, if you must know. But you're already doing so much, and . . ."

"It's really not a problem. I can fit it in with my own grocery shopping. The children can come with me. I'd enjoy it. Actually," she laughed softly, "I love to cook, and I don't get the opportunity to do it for others very often. My cat won't eat anything unless it has tuna in it."

Mr. Brynner chuckled. "I'll leave some money on top of the fridge for you. I trust your judgment. And thanks again."

The following day, Helen found an envelope on the fridge with a hundred dollars cash in it. She had the children help her plan a menu for a week, including meals for the weekend that their father could handle. They made a list, then went shopping. She dropped her own groceries off at her house and the children met Twinkle, who eagerly lapped up their attention. Returning to the apartment, she put a significant amount of change back in the envelope, then they proceeded to make chicken enchiladas, putting enough cooked chicken in the freezer to use for two other recipes.

The weekend seemed longer than usual to Helen, but she enjoyed her Primary class on Sunday, and looked forward to Monday with the extra purpose her life had gained. She was so delighted to see Scotty and Tamara again that she began to wonder what she would do when their mother returned, as Mr. Brynner had said she would. Helen had wondered more than once if her illness was terminal, but he seemed to intimate that all of this was temporary.

With a casserole in the oven and the school work done, Helen helped the children tidy their rooms. She found that there were not great quantities of toys and clothing, but what they had was nice without being extravagant. Then she realized that the apartment had only two bedrooms, and each of the children had one, with a twin bed. Each room had several boxes stacked neatly out of the way, as if they hadn't completely finished unpacking from the move. Scotty's room, the larger of the two, had an extra dresser and some of his father's things in the closet.

"Where does your father sleep?" Helen asked casually.

"On the couch," Tamara answered. "It unfolds into a bed. Daddy sold the brass bed that Mom bought. He said he liked the couch better."

Helen just nodded and changed the subject, wondering again over the specifics of this situation, but reminding herself that it was none of her business. On Tuesday they went together to the laundromat, then worked together to put all of the laundry away. On Wednesday they cleaned out the fridge and made cookies. On Thursday they organized the kitchen cupboards. She had to deal with some occasional fighting and bad behavior between the children, but as she established boundaries and stuck to them, it gradually eased up.

On Friday, they made a chore chart and learned how to make their beds. Helen usually had supper ready early enough so that she could eat with the children, then she set some out for their father when he returned home. But he came home a little early on Friday, just as they were setting the table. He insisted that she stay and eat with them, and she listened quietly as the children shared the happenings of the day with him. Occasionally the adults exchanged a smile in mutual appreciation of some funny or sweet comment. As soon as the meal was finished, Mr. Brynner insisted that he would clean up, and Helen was on her way home.

Through another long weekend, Helen kept busy by catching up on her own laundry, cleaning out her own fridge, and spending time with Twinkle. She went shopping with Carla on Saturday afternoon. On Sunday evening, she went to a fireside with another single sister in her ward.

Monday afternoon, she helped the children prepare a home evening lesson to share with their father, and on Tuesday she had them ready to go trick-or-treating when their father got home. Mr. Brynner looked skeptically at the comical witch dress she had worn to school, made from a black fabric covered with orange cats. But it was the plastic warts she'd glued on her nose and chin that seemed to really catch his attention. He smirked and thanked her profusely as he always did, then she went home to greet the trick-or-treaters in her own neighborhood while Twinkle slept in her favorite corner of the couch.

With November came the realization that, having the apartment in good order and the children doing their chores to keep it that way, they were all prone to boredom. Helen took them to a museum and the fire station, and she helped with one of Scotty's Cub Scout meetings when the assistant den leader got sick.

She took them to the library more than once, and together they read many stories. Helen had almost forgotten that these children had a mother until Tamara commented one afternoon, "I like it when you read to us. Mom never read to us."

The children didn't talk about their mother often, and when they did, it was usually with very little emotion. Of course, Helen reminded herself that she wasn't around them enough to get an accurate picture of their feelings. Occasionally, they said they missed their mother, and once Scotty even cried over her absence while Tamara was busy in her bedroom. Helen wondered if their mother's illness had prevented her from being involved with the children as much as she would have liked. She felt a deep compassion for Mrs. Brynner, wherever she might be. It must be very difficult, she thought, to be separated from these adorable children for so long. But as always, with thoughts of their mother, Helen wondered when the woman might return and force Helen back to her old way of life. Looking back over the brief time she'd been helping the Brynner family, she wondered how she had ever managed without having them in her life. Scotty and Tamara had become so comfortable with her that they'd begun calling her Helen, which suited her fine— although she stipulated that at school they must obey the rules and still refer to her as Miss Star in order to set a good example for the other children.

While her students cut out brightly colored construction-paper feathers for their Thanksgiving turkeys, Helen was pleased to realize that Scotty was doing much better in school, and having recently talked with Tamara's teacher, it was evident that she was also doing well.

That evening, while Helen was preparing tacos, the phone rang. Only then did it occur to her that it almost never did. The children didn't seem to have any serious playmates beyond some children who lived next door and came over to play occasionally, and no one else ever called. The children ignored the phone, so Helen picked it up; but after she'd said hello, she wondered if she should have just let the machine answer it.

"Who's this?" a woman's voice asked.

"This is the sitter. May I help you?"

"I guess Shayne's not there, then."

For a moment Helen was certain the caller had reached a wrong number. Then she realized that she'd never heard Mr. Brynner's first name. "No," was all she said.

"Let me talk to Scotty, then," the woman said tersely.

"Scotty," Helen called, "the phone is for you."

Scotty reluctantly turned his attention from *Arthur* and came to the phone. "Hi, Mom," he said, and Helen couldn't help being curious. She was amazed at his lack of enthusiasm. He made a few grunts and answered "yes" and "no" before he called Tamara to the phone. She sounded a bit more enthusiastic about talking to her mother, but there was a subtle affectation to her voice. It was as if little Tamara actually had the insight to try to sound pleased for her mother's benefit, even though she wasn't. The impression left on Helen was less than favorable, but she reminded herself not to jump to conclusions.

When Mr. Brynner came home, Helen informed him of the call while she was shredding cheese. "Your wife called," she mentioned casually.

"Thank you," he said, and turned toward the phone. "I was hoping you wouldn't have eaten yet," he added. "It's nice to eat together." The comment made Helen wonder if she'd been insensitive to eat with the children most of the time before he returned home. She wondered if she should just prepare their meal and eat discreetly, or just take a portion home. She was startled when he continued. "You will be staying to eat with us, won't you? The children seem so much happier when you're here."

"I'd love to, but . . . I don't want to overstep my bounds, or—"

"Don't be silly," he said with a little laugh as he dialed a long-distance number and turned his attention to the phone.

Helen couldn't help overhearing his side of the conversation; but then, she figured if he'd wanted privacy he could have used the extension in Scotty's bedroom. Of course, he didn't say much more than Scotty had: one-word answers to questions and some occasional grunting, as if to indicate he was listening. But she did notice that his tone of voice changed dramatically through the course of the five-minute call. He'd started out with an exuberant "Hello, darling, how are you feeling?" and he finished with a hollow, resigned, "Will you be coming home for Thanksgiving? Well, I see. Perhaps Christmas, then."

For a full minute after he hung up the phone, Shayne Brynner stared at the floor, seeming lost and alone. Helen asked him a question that he obviously didn't hear. She waited for a long moment, then touched his arm. "Excuse me, Mr. Brynner, are you—"

"Please, call me Shayne," he said with a forced smile.

"Very well," she said. "Are you ready to eat? It's on the table."

"Of course," he said, then he became distant again.

"Forgive me," she said. "I couldn't help overhearing. Is Mrs. Brynner not well enough to come home for Thanksgiving?"

"I seriously doubt that's a problem," he said, almost under his breath and with a subtle snarl.

While Helen had imagined his wife to be seriously ill, even dying, she found his comment suddenly disconcerting. Obviously there was more to this situation than met the eye, but she reminded herself that it was none of her business. "Forgive me," she said. "I shouldn't pry. I just—"

"You're not prying, Miss Starkey," he said, seeming more like himself, although his tone had a subtle bite. "You have every right to be aware of the circumstances here, when you have been more of a mother to these children than their own mother ever was." He stopped as if he'd caught himself, and chuckled tensely. "Forgive me; I shouldn't vent my frustration on you. You really should know what's happening, if only so you can help the children understand. But it's difficult to talk about, and . . ."

He was interrupted as the children finished what they'd been doing and realized supper was on the table. Helen noticed that on the surface he seemed unaffected by the phone call, but having gotten to know him a little better, she could see in his eyes that he was deeply troubled. The meal passed with bits of small talk interjected into lengths of silence. After the children had finished and rinsed off their plates, they went to the front room to play *Sorry*, a board game that Helen had brought from home.

While Shayne helped Helen clear the table, she sensed that he needed to talk but likely wouldn't. Not wanting to be pushy, she simply said, "Forgive me for asking, but is it not possible for you and the children to travel in order to be with . . ."

"Margie," he provided.

"Margie," she said, "for Thanksgiving?"

"No," he said, "it's not possible."

She assumed there wasn't enough money to make the trip, and made no further comment.

"My aunt will be coming for Thanksgiving," he said. "She always brightens things up a bit."

When it became evident the subject wouldn't be brought up again, Helen made her usual exit after he'd refused her offer to wash the dishes.

Thanksgiving break seemed especially long and tedious for Helen. She enjoyed having dinner with a family in her ward, and she talked on the phone with her parents and brothers, but she went to bed early Thursday evening. She was incredibly relieved when Shayne Brynner called her the next morning.

"I've had sort of an emergency come up at work," he said. "I'm going to have to put in a long day. I hate to interrupt your vacation, but is there any possible way you could take the children today? I'll make it up to you, I promise."

"I'd love to," she agreed eagerly. "And you don't have to make it up to me. I have some things I need to do at home, but I'd love to have them over."

Shayne dropped the children off ten minutes after she gave him her address. They were still in their pajamas and hadn't eaten yet, but Helen quickly mixed up some pancakes and made animals and letters with the batter on the grill. Their response to the simple breakfast made her feel as if she'd taken them to Disneyland.

While Helen spiffed up the kitchen, the children used the spare bedrooms to get dressed and pack their pajamas into the bags they'd brought with them. They watched a Disney video while Helen did her much-needed housecleaning—a drudgery that seemed to take on a new purpose with having children under the roof.

They went to the grocery store and bought toothbrushes for Scotty and Tamara, since they'd forgotten to bring them along and they'd not yet brushed their teeth. Then they cooked supper together, making the chicken enchiladas that the children had declared they loved when she'd made them before. "They don't have any icky green things in 'em," Scotty declared. "Just chicken and good stuff."

After the kitchen was cleaned up, they played games, read stories, and played with Twinkle until Shayne came to get them later in the evening. Helen sent home a plate of food that he could heat in the microwave, and he brought the children again the next morning. As Helen contemplated his need to work such long hours on a Saturday, she asked the children some questions and realized that he worked Saturdays about half the time, and when he did they usually stayed with a woman who lived in their ward. "She's nice, but not as nice as you," Scotty observed.

"You're more fun, too," Tamara said. "And she couldn't tend us on school days because she works at the city building."

Thinking further on it, Helen realized that she had no idea what Shayne Brynner's occupation was. Asking a few more questions, she came to the conclusion that it was some kind of construction, although it had nothing to do with building homes.

In spite of knowing the crowds would be horrible, Helen took the children to a mall, where they admired the elaborate Christmas decorations and sampled treats from a number of different shops. She made a mental note to ask Shayne about the possibility of allowing her to help them do some Christmas shopping for their parents—and anyone else they might need to get gifts for.

They stopped and had a hamburger and fries on the way home. The children were especially silly, but they easily calmed down when Helen gently reminded them to be polite. She was just thinking what good children they were when Tamara said, "Mom used to get mad at us when we laughed. She didn't like us to laugh."

The statement was startling to Helen, but she only said, "Maybe she didn't feel well, honey."

The children said nothing more. In fact they became especially quiet. Helen broke the tension by saying, "You like hamburgers, I see."

"Yeah," Scotty said, "we used to have them all the time before Mom left. I didn't like 'em all the time, but since we haven't had one for a long time, I think it tastes good."

"I think so, too," Tamara said.

They returned to Helen's house to find a message on her answering machine that Shayne would be late. He said to call his cell phone if there was a problem. Helen had had the number for weeks, but she'd never had the need to use it. And tonight she was only too glad to have the children's company a while longer. They got ready for bed and brushed their teeth with the new toothbrushes that Helen had left in a special place for them to use at her house.

By the time Shayne arrived, Tamara was sound asleep on the couch with an afghan tucked around her, and Scotty was getting sleepy. Helen answered the door to find an exhausted- looking father with concern in his eyes. "I'm so sorry to do this to you two days in a row," he said.

"We had a great time," she insisted. "But you obviously didn't. Come in."

"Thank you," he said after he'd made certain his boots wouldn't track any dirt into the house. "We had a main water line burst yesterday morning, and we've been pumping water and assessing damages. It's been a real mess."

"You do construction, right?"

"Yes," he said. "Industrial." He said nothing more, and she figured he must consider one word enough of a description of his work. "How were the children?" he asked, following her into the family room just off the kitchen. Helen had always disliked the technical name of the room—until the last couple of days.

"They were fine," she said. "I'm afraid Tamara's asleep, and Scotty's not far off."

Shayne smiled warmly when he saw them, and his tenderness as he scooped Tamara into his arms was evident.

"Just take the afghan," Helen said. "I'll get it Monday."

"Thank you again," he said. She followed him out to his truck, guiding Scotty and carrying their bags.

Helen stood on the sidewalk long after the truck had disappeared around the corner. She imagined Shayne Brynner tucking his children into their beds and kissing their little foreheads, and she wished that she could do the same. Then she sighed and went back into the house, grateful to at least have Twinkle there to meet her at the door.

CHILDREN-FRIENDLY CHICKEN ENCHILADAS

1 can cream of chicken soup
1 can milk
1 small carton sour cream (8 oz.)
12 flour tortillas
Cooked chunks of chicken
Sliced black olives
Shredded cheddar cheese

Mix soup, milk, and sour cream. Spread a little soup mixture on bottom of a 9" x 13" pan. Spread some soup mixture down center of each tortilla, along with some cheese, chicken, and olives. Roll tortillas and place in pan. Spread remaining mixture over top and then shredded cheese. Bake at 375° until hot.

No need to pick out the icky green stuff.

Chapter 3

Shayne Brynner tucked his children into bed, then dragged his exhausted body into a hot shower. He didn't know what suddenly made him more emotional than he had dared to be for months, maybe years. Maybe it was the reality of another holiday passing without Margie here. Maybe it was the approach of Christmas. Maybe it was the sheer physical and emotional exhaustion that suddenly became too much. Whatever the reason, he was surprised by the surge of tears that overtook him. He pressed his face to the cold shower wall and let the hot water run over his head as he cried like a baby until the water turned cool, then he forced himself to calm down and check on the children.

Watching their sweet faces lost in the oblivion of sleep, he wondered if they ever cried over their mother's absence when he wasn't aware. Or if they held it inside the way he had been doing until tonight. He thought of asking Helen what she might have observed, and wished it wasn't too late to call her.

Settling himself into his bed in the front room, he recalled that he'd forgotten his prayers. Too tired to get out of bed, he closed his eyes and willed his silent words heavenward. Many of his pleas had been the same for months, or was it years? But even though certain things hadn't changed, and some had gotten worse, he could see the evidence that he was being looked after. And one of those blessings had come in the form of Helen Starkey. He wondered what he would have done without her all these weeks. She seemed to be tangible proof that his Heavenly Father was mindful of him. Like a single star against an otherwise black sky, her genuine caring on behalf of his children meant more to him than he could ever say. He smiled to himself at his analogy. "Miss Star," he said into the darkness. Then he drifted off to sleep.

Sunday was typically difficult as he got himself and the children to church, almost on time. He knew the ward members meant well, but every inquiry about Margie and her health seemed to tighten the muscles in his back and the knots in his stomach. He was glad that he'd been able to find an apartment within the same ward boundaries; it had helped with the transition. But he wondered what these people would think if they knew the truth about his wife and the circumstances they were in as a result of her struggles.

It was nice to get home from meetings and know that dinner would be hot in the oven, thanks to the casserole Helen had left in the freezer with simple instructions that she had taped to it. Even without being there, she seemed to somehow soften the harsh effects of Margie's absence. But then, even when Margie had been at home, things had not been much different. At least now he wasn't expecting anything of her—only clinging to some futile hope that she would come back and make things right.

Late in the afternoon, the children started chattering about what Santa might bring them for Christmas. Under the circumstances, the thought of celebrating the biggest holiday of the year made Shayne feel cold inside. He couldn't comprehend doing it without Margie, and he wondered how to go about getting gifts and decorating the apartment. Christmas was one thing Margie had enjoyed and participated in, and he didn't know if he could manage. Perhaps Helen could give him some suggestions, he concluded. Then he put it out of his mind.

Two weeks later he was still managing to put it out of his mind, while an impending disaster seemed to threaten what little stability he'd been trying to hold on to. His phone calls with Margie were becoming less frequent and her attitude more abrupt. For years he'd locked away his disappointments and struggles, just fighting to keep the family together and cope with day-to-day living. And when she finally did what she'd been threatening to do for years, he'd hung on to the hope that she would see what he considered obvious and come home; that they could be a family. But time was passing, and something deep inside urged him to face the possibility that she might not ever come back. Except that he could hardly bear to think of it. How could he face it? How would the children face it? What would he possibly do? How could he handle the impact this would have on the children? And for some reason, the coming of Christmas seemed to somehow force him to look at the situation realistically. Each time he talked to Margie, she said she would be home for Christmas. But there was something in her voice that made him believe she was only pacifying him—that she was putting off something inevitable. And he was scared.

"I'll see you for Christmas, then," he said into the phone one evening as Helen was preparing supper. He couldn't help feeling as if he was lying to himself as well as to Margie. How long had they been playing these games?

"Yes," his wife answered as if he'd done something wrong.

He quickly concluded the conversation and hung up the phone as he glanced toward the calendar, noting that the holiday was getting close. He felt so unprepared—on every count.

"Are you all right?" Helen's voice startled him from his thoughts.

Shayne turned to look at her and nearly lied, but he couldn't bring himself to say anything. When he said nothing, she added, "Will Margie be coming home for Christmas?"

"That's what she keeps telling me," he said. "But she was going to come home for Halloween and Thanksgiving, too."

Helen watched Shayne closely, wondering how to approach the problem. She didn't want to say or do anything inappropriate, but instinctively she believed she was here to make a difference for this little family. She was about to open the subject up when the children came in for supper. They sat together to eat, mostly in silence. It was as if Scotty and Tamara sensed their father's discouragement, even though he did well at covering it in their presence.

"This meat loaf is wonderful," Shayne said with enthusiasm, breaking a long stretch of silence.

"Me and Scotty squished it," Tamara said proudly.

"And it's not a meat *loaf,*" Scotty clarified. "It's a meat *ring.*" He quoted Helen accurately as he repeated her reasoning. "If you bake it in a round pan and leave a hole in the middle, it gets cooked all the way through without getting dried out."

"Very good," Shayne said to Scotty, winking discreetly at Helen. "Miss Star is teaching both of you to be excellent cooks."

Helen smiled, and the meal was finished in silence. After they'd eaten and rinsed their dishes, the children went back to putting a puzzle together in the front room. While Helen cleared the table, she felt strongly that the man still seated there, staring into nothing, needed very much to talk. She recalled a conversation some weeks earlier, during which he'd admitted that perhaps she could help the children if she knew what was going on. That conversation had been interrupted and never brought up again. But now, as she sat back down across from him, it was evident the problem was no small thing. She uttered a silent prayer and said quietly, "I know I'm just the nanny-slash-housekeeper, but if you'd like to talk, I'm willing to listen. Maybe it would help me help the children if I knew a little of what's happening. Only if you want to, of course. I haven't wanted to be nosy, but—"

"Nosy?" He chuckled tensely. "You are the most un-nosy person I have ever known. To be truthful, I was hoping you would have pried it out of me a long time ago. I'm concerned for the children in a way that I can't even begin to express. I know next to nothing about the psychological impact of such difficulties on children, but I'm certain it can't be good. Perhaps you, with your expertise, could help me out."

"Well, I don't know that I'm so good with psychology, but—"

"But you are an expert with children."

"I suppose I am. And I can tell you that they are incredibly resilient. I doubt there is much I could teach you. You give them love and acceptance. You give them appropriate discipline and firm boundaries . . . from what I've observed, at least. They're really fairly well-adjusted children."

"Really?" he asked, seeming so pleasantly surprised that Helen felt a little emotional.

"Really," she said.

He seemed lost in thought until she startled him out of it. "Mr. Brynner, if there is something I can—"

"I told you to call me Shayne."

"Very well," she smiled. "Shayne. If there is something I can do to help with regard to the children, all you have to do is ask."

He watched her closely for a long moment, as if he was contemplating something, then he said, "I'm grateful for your offer, and . . . I would like to talk, but . . ." He hesitated and seemed nervous somehow. "Miss Starkey . . . Helen, you have been more than wonderful, but . . ."

Helen's heart began to pound. Would he tell her that she had overstepped her bounds? Would he tell her not to come back? How could she bear being without the children when she'd grown so close to them?

"Forgive me," he said, "I don't know how to say this any way except bluntly. It's lovely to have you stay and eat with us, but . . . perhaps it's more appropriate if we . . . talk under some other circumstances. On the phone, maybe. I don't know that any of my neighbors would be keeping track of the time between my arrival and your leaving each evening. But whether they are or not, I don't want to put you, or myself, into any situation that anyone would construe as inappropriate. On behalf of my children, I need you. And I'm hoping you'll be willing to continue helping them as you have been. But we must be careful. Am I sounding like a total idiot, or am I making any sense?"

"Making sense, actually," she said, relieved that he wasn't going to ask her to discontinue her help with the children. She couldn't help but respect him for his insight and his desire to maintain total propriety in their relationship. While her thoughts and feelings had never strayed toward anything inappropriate, she'd never stopped to consider that the situation might not be. Perhaps that's because she wasn't married, and she'd never had to think in such a vein. Sensing that he was embarrassed and uncertain, she stood and said lightly, "I'd best be on my way, so I'll leave you to wash the dishes and . . . well, feel free to call me if you need some advice, or . . . perhaps we could have a little parent-teacher conference at the school."

Shayne smiled, betraying the full extent of his relief that she'd not misunderstood him. A few days passed while Helen wondered if he would ever take the opportunity to seek out her help and advice. Everything went on as it had before. She managed to have supper on about the time he got home. He would insist that she sit and eat with them, but she was always out the door less than twenty minutes after his arrival. And Helen felt certain that whether or not anyone took notice of their comings and goings, it was better for them to know that in his wife's absence, nothing could even appear inappropriate.

"So," Carla asked over lunch, three days after Shayne's request, "do you think his wife is dying or something?"

"I suppose it's possible, but I don't think so. It seems more complicated. I don't doubt that she has some kind of health problem, but it's much more than that. I've tried to speculate too much. It's really none of my business. But I do want to help the children."

"Scotty's doing much better, isn't he?" Carla asked, helping herself to Helen's fresh cauliflower and ranch dip.

"Oh, much better. He's thriving, actually. And Tamara's doing well, too. But their father seems concerned for reasons I don't understand. I guess that's what he wants to talk to me about, but he's sure taking his time getting around to it. Of course, he's very busy, but . . ." She left the sentence unfinished when another teacher sat down too close to keep their conversation confidential.

The afternoon dragged more than usual for Helen. While the children glued cotton balls on paper Santa Claus faces, she contemplated how deeply she had grown to care for Scotty and Tamara, and the respect she had gained for their father. She turned her attention to the snow falling outside, while in her heart she prayed that the Brynner family would be reunited and they could all be incomparably happy. But at the same time, she hoped that the return of Mrs. Brynner would not leave her out in the cold. Perhaps, with her ill health, they could still use her help. Perhaps she and Margie Brynner could become friends. That was a pleasant thought.

Helen was drawn away from her thoughts by some teasing that was getting out of hand. She sighed and went to deal with it, hoping the remaining hour of the school day would go quickly.

⊰❋⊱

Shayne ran from his truck through the snow toward the main school doors. Once inside, he brushed the snow out of his hair and glanced at his watch. He hurried toward the office, but the little school map on the wall just outside the office door saved him from having to ask directions. He easily found his way, feeling a sudden onslaught of nerves when he saw the bright yellow star on the wall beside an open door. *Miss Star, Grade 3,* the little sign read. Pausing for a moment to absorb the little pictures of snowmen hanging along the hallway, he smiled when he found Scotty's and briefly admired his son's artistic abilities.

Shayne glanced at his watch, but avoided going anywhere near the door where she might see him. He'd wanted to get here before class let out to be certain he didn't miss her. He knew that she would be an ally in helping the children through whatever might lie ahead, and he understood that it was important to tell her the whole story. But he'd never told anyone the *whole* story before. And just thinking about it tied his stomach in knots. He hoped she would have the time to talk with him. Perhaps he should have warned her; maybe he should have made an appointment. He'd simply taken advantage of the bad weather giving him the afternoon off, but he hadn't thought it through very carefully.

The bell's ringing scared him nearly to death. Then, suddenly, all was chaos. Children streamed out of every door, and it occurred to him that anyone would have to be gifted to deal with so many youngsters every single day. Once Miss Star's room seemed to be cleared out, he stepped tentatively into the doorway. A quick glance told him she was sitting at her desk on the opposite side of the room. His son was sitting on the floor near a colorful bookshelf, absorbed in a book.

Shayne took a deep breath and readied himself to enter and approach her. Then he took notice of the room, and his nerves suddenly calmed as he became distracted by the stars. There were stars everywhere. It was like the schoolroom from heaven. There were star mobiles and star wind chimes. Star fabric was arranged strategically around the three large windows, as well as framing the bulletin board where a child's picture was featured as *Star of the Week*. There were star knick-knacks, and an apron covered with stars hung from a hook on the wall. And in the middle of it all was Miss Star, wearing a necklace of wooden stars over her green sweater.

Reminding himself of his purpose, he took a deep breath and moved toward the desk, praying this would go well.

Helen looked up when she noticed movement, and she felt a little nervous flutter as Shayne Brynner entered her classroom. She'd never seen him dressed in anything but work clothes before. He'd obviously gone home to clean up before coming. She wondered if this was the "parent-teacher conference" she'd been waiting for.

"Well, look who's here," she said, and Scotty looked up.

"Daddy!" he said, running to hug his father.

"Hello there, Scooter," he said, and a moment later Tamara came into the room and gave him the same reaction. After he had greeted the children, he said, "Would you have a few minutes to talk, Miss Star? Or is this a bad time?"

"No, now is fine. If you'll just excuse me for a moment. I'll be right back."

Helen hurried across the hall to find Carla alone in her classroom. She moved close beside her and said quietly, "He's here."

"Here?" Carla asked, as if he was a celebrity or something.

"He wants to talk, so . . . could the kids come over here while you're finishing up? I think it might . . . well, you know . . ."

"Yes, I know," she said, "and it's not a problem. I'm going to be here for at least an hour. But I want to see this guy."

"What for? He's just a guy."

"And I'm just curious."

"Fine. But be casual."

Helen returned to her room with Carla close behind. "Hey guys," Carla said to the children while she glanced discreetly at their father, "why don't you come over here for a little while. I've got some pictures that are in desperate need of coloring."

"Go along," Helen said when they looked to her as if for permission. "Your father and I are going to talk for a few minutes."

After the children left with Carla, leaving the door open, Helen sat at her desk and invited Shayne to sit across from her, just as she would during any parent-teacher conference. "So," she said with exaggerated formality, "what can I do for you, Mr. Brynner?"

He chuckled, and the tension eased somewhat. A moment later he cleared his throat and began, "Well, I'll get right to the point. I'm simply concerned about helping the children understand the situation with their mother, without . . . how shall I say it? Well, I don't want to give them a negative impression of their mother. They have a right to love her and look up to her. On the other hand, I want to be honest with them; otherwise, they could grow up very confused. Am I making any sense?"

"I believe so," she said, realizing more clearly that this situation had a lot more to it than simply his wife's poor health. When he didn't continue, she said, "I know your wife is ill, and I'm only assuming that your need to move had something to do with . . . related struggles."

She saw his face tighten into a scowl and wondered if she had said something out of line. "Perhaps I should start at the beginning, Miss Starkey, unless you're in a hurry or—"

"I'm not in a hurry," she said. "And my name is Helen."

"Helen," he said, leaning back in his chair.

"My wife has a heart condition," Shayne began. "It was discovered in her early childhood. When we were dating, I was well aware that she had to take certain precautions, and it was something she was keenly aware of. But it didn't seem to stop her from doing what she wanted to do, and I had every reason to believe she was strong and managing her condition well. When we got married, something seemed to change in her—almost overnight. She quit her job, then she quit school. We weren't married in the temple, for reasons I've never fully understood, so I won't try to explain. But her promise to be sealed seemed quickly forgotten as soon as she had that ring on her finger.

"She complained continually about her health, and did practically nothing around the house. Of course I was concerned, figuring her health had taken a turn for the worse. But more than one doctor assured me that her condition was not severe, and if she would take care of herself appropriately, she could live a full and productive life. Her obstetrician felt certain that pregnancy would not be a problem as long as she took care of herself."

"Go on," Helen said when he hesitated.

"Well, having the kids was hard on her, but once she recovered it was determined that her heart condition had not worsened, and she was in good health. Still, through the years the situation has only escalated. I . . ." He paused abruptly and gave her a sharp glance.

"Is something wrong?" she asked.

"Only that . . . well, I've never been one to whine and complain. I've always done my best to face up to my problems and solve them effectively. Perhaps that's why this is so difficult to talk about."

"I'm just listening, Shayne. I'm not going to pass any judgments. If you want my opinion, you should have been talking about this to someone a long time ago. Don't you have anyone you can talk to?"

"Not really," he admitted. "My parents are on a mission, and my siblings are spread out around the country. I guess I could talk to any one of them, but . . . well, maybe I've never wanted to admit to the family how my marriage really is. But my only concern here and now is for the children." Helen waited quietly for him to continue. He sighed and looked down. "I think I was in denial for a very long time. We'd argue now and then about the problem. She'd tell me I was unsympathetic to her condition, that I had no idea what it was like to have her health problems. I talked to doctors. I took her in for physicals regularly. I tried to learn and understand. But the problem only got worse."

"Forgive me," Helen said, "but I'm a little unclear about . . . the problem."

Shayne sighed and looked around. "Well," he said, "it all happened so gradually that it's difficult to say exactly when and how it happened. But the reality I have been dealing with for quite some time now is . . . well . . . Margie will not cook. She will not clean. She will not do grocery shopping. She's gifted at buying fast food, no matter the cost. She will shop at malls and department stores, as if spending money on herself was somehow a remedy for her ailment. I can't count how many times I sat down with her and pleaded concerning our financial situation. She just told me I was unsympathetic to her condition and didn't understand. I finally had to call the credit card companies and have the accounts closed. She was furious. The situation got so bad last summer that I realized we could never make the house payments and handle all the debts while she continued to spend as much as she could get her hands on. Then she would lie around for days at a time, complaining all the while that the children gave her a headache and she was too ill to do anything."

While Shayne showed varying degrees of anger and frustration, Helen listened with growing amazement as the picture became perfectly, logically, and appallingly clear.

He sighed again and folded his arms over his chest. "I'm not trying to justify myself, Helen. I am far from perfect. But I know in my heart that I tried everything in my power to rectify the problem and work it out reasonably. I would usually come home from work and cook supper if she hadn't already picked up hamburgers or had a pizza delivered. I did laundry. I cleaned house. But it was never enough. When I told her we would have to put the house up for sale, she told me I was just going to have go out and find a way to make more money. My income is more than adequate, Helen. I'm a supervisor, and my wage is better than average for my line of work. When I reminded her of this, she insisted that we just declare bankruptcy and start over."

Helen resisted the urge to allow her mouth to hang open. She could hardly believe what she was hearing. But she said nothing and motioned for him to go on.

"Well, I refused. Plain and simple. I told her I would do whatever I had to to pay back every penny of the debts she had incurred, and she was going to have to live with the consequences of her actions. If that meant living in a tiny apartment until we got a handle on the situation, so be it. When the house actually sold, she left. She told me that I was—"

"Let me guess," Helen said. "Unsympathetic to her condition, and you didn't understand."

"Exactly," he said and leaned forward. "I have analyzed this until my head hurts. I have prayed and fasted and struggled to understand. And it came to me one night while I was studying the scriptures." He quoted the verse firmly. "'Therefore shall a man leave his father and his mother, and shall cleave unto his wife; and they shall be one flesh.'" He took a deep breath. "You see, Helen, Margie never let go of the way her parents coddled her because of her heart condition. I look back now and realize there were some warning signs when we were dating, but it's easy to rationalize that everything will get better once you're married. Well, it didn't. I had hoped that moving her away from her family would make it better, and I knew in my heart that the move to Utah was right. But it only made things worse. She was never able to let go. And now she's gone back to her mother, and I believe she's convinced that with her mother is where she belongs. She's convinced that her health problems are beyond my comprehension, in spite of my continual efforts to study the problem and support her."

He paused, and Helen didn't know what to say. She was glad when he continued, "Now, as I was saying, I told her I would do whatever was necessary to put our finances in order. I could see the path we were on, and we weren't going to make it. So I put the house up for sale. Fortunately, none of the mortgage papers had her name on them. She'd wanted nothing to do with the business of buying the house initially; she just wanted to live in it. She was furious when I put it on the market, and she was so difficult about showing it that I was afraid it wouldn't sell before it went into foreclosure. But we were blessed with a miracle. Some wonderful people made an offer and the sale went through relatively fast. That's when Margie suddenly became more ill than she ever had been, even though she refused to see a doctor. She declared that I had never been sympathetic to her condition. She'd had enough, and she was going home where her mother could take care of her. I had really hoped that once she was away for a while, she would come to her senses, and realize that being a family was more important than money, or illness, or where we live, or anything. But it's becoming increasingly evident that I was wrong."

When it seemed he was finished, Helen said, "So your financial situation is obviously a problem, since—"

"Actually," he interrupted, "we're fine now. Selling the house made it possible to pay off the majority of the debts she had run up. We had a big yard sale after Margie left, and got rid of a lot of the superfluous things she'd been collecting that just took up space. We have quite a bit of Margie's stuff in boxes. I didn't get rid of anything personal or sentimental, of course." He said it as if he believed that sooner or later he would have to adamantly defend himself on that count. "Right now we're debt-free, and I'm saving up for a down payment. We'll start over in a year or so and be just fine."

"That's great," Helen said. "About the money, I mean."

"Yes, all things considered, we've been very blessed, but . . ." His voice trailed off, and the reality of the situation showed blatantly in his eyes. "I keep trying to tell myself that she'll come back and we'll be able to be a family. It's what I'm hoping and praying for with every fiber of my being. But there's a part of me that's having a hard time believing it will happen. I apologize for rambling on this way, Helen. Maybe it's not completely appropriate, but . . . I consider you a friend. And I'm concerned for the children."

"Well, your concern is certainly understandable," she said. "From what I've observed, they seem to be adjusting rather well, but—"

"Thanks to you," Shayne said. "They've become so much more even tempered since you came along—especially Scotty. Those first few weeks after Margie left, they were constantly fighting, whining for their mother, and just being generally difficult. I think that's why we had a hard time keeping baby-sitters. Quite frankly, you've been a great blessing to us. And I'm not afraid to admit that the children need you to get through whatever may come of this. Whether Margie comes back or not, there are going to be some difficult adjustments."

"I'll do anything I can," Helen said, hoping that his wife's return wouldn't mean that she would be pushed out of the picture completely. But she had no problem saying, "I truly hope your family can be put back together, and whatever happens, I'm certain the children will come through just fine. Don't forget that they have a good father who gives them a lot of love and security." He glanced away as if he didn't quite believe her, and she added, "I appreciate your being candid with me. I'll try to be aware of their feelings, and if I observe anything that might be a concern, I'll let you know."

"Thank you," he said, rising to leave. He looked so tall; but then, compared to the average height of the third-graders who usually occupied the room, he was.

Helen felt the need to say, "I'll be praying for you . . . all of you. I'm certain that everything will work out."

He chuckled tensely and added, "What I need is a miracle, I suppose."

"Well, I would think you certainly deserve one." Again he looked surprised, and she added, "Maybe she'll come home for Christmas, and everything will improve."

"Maybe," he said with a barely detectable quiver in his voice. "Thank you again." He walked toward the door, then turned back, "Uh . . . I'll just take the children with me. I have the rest of the day off, and thought I might take them Christmas shopping."

Helen smiled, but she couldn't help feeling a little disappointed. "I'll see you tomorrow, then," she said, and followed him to Carla's room where the children were playing a counting game with wooden beads.

After they had left, Carla said, "Wow, he's adorable."

Helen turned toward her, startled. It was the last thing she'd expected to hear. "He's a very good man," she replied.

"Yes," Carla said, "and he's adorable."

Helen shrugged. "I suppose he is. And he's also married."

"I wasn't implying anything," Carla said. "It was just a comment."

Helen shrugged again, finding herself distracted by the story he'd just told her. It was difficult to believe that a woman could be so intolerable. She was startled when Carla added, "So, what's the scoop? Or is it private?"

"Well, it's private beyond me and my best friend."

"Okay, so let's go get a hot fudge sundae and you can bounce it off me, since you apparently have the afternoon off."

Helen appreciated Carla's insight. She did feel the need to talk all of this through, if only to make sense of it with regard to helping the children, as he'd requested. She had no doubt that her conversation with Carla would be kept completely confidential, and she did need a sounding board.

Long after their sundaes were finished, Helen and Carla sat in a corner booth of the ice cream parlor and discussed the situation. She realized that the extra time she'd been spending with the children had given her less time with Carla. Of course, Carla was very busy with her family, so she doubted that her friend had even noticed. After Helen had described the things she'd observed and repeated everything she'd been told this afternoon, Carla just shook her head. "That's unbelievable," she said. "When people like you and me are trying so hard to do what's right and make a positive difference in the world, it's hard to imagine that a grown woman could be such a baby."

"Yes, it is," Helen agreed.

"Listen," Carla said, "you've probably already thought of this, but I just have to say it. You know as well as I do, from many things that have come up through our years of teaching, that there are always two sides of a coin. I'm not saying you shouldn't believe what he's told you; there's no reason not to. But keep an open mind. You've never even talked to this Margie woman beyond 'Hello, I'll get the kids' over the phone.

So just . . . well . . . you know . . . take it with a grain of salt, as they say."

"I will, yes, thank you. That thought had crossed my mind. As you say, I have no reason to believe he's not trustworthy, but I've learned not to judge and jump to conclusions."

That night, Helen had trouble sleeping. Shayne Brynner's story kept playing through her mind. She wondered about the day-to-day difficulties that he and the children had faced through the years, and she couldn't help admiring his love and concern for his children. She prayed that she *would* be able to help the children through whatever lay ahead, and she prayed that the Brynner family would indeed get their miracle.

MEAT RING—NOT LOAF

1 1/2 lbs. ground beef
3/4 cup oatmeal or cracker crumbs
1/4 cup finely chopped onion
1 1/2 teaspoon salt
1/4 teaspoon pepper
1 beaten egg
3/4 cup milk

Mix all together and mold into round pan, leaving a hole in the center.
Cover with sauce and bake 1 hour at 350°.

Sauce: *1/3 cup ketchup*
2 tablespoons brown sugar
1 tablespoon mustard

Chapter 4

The following day when Helen took the children to the apartment, she found a note from Shayne, asking her if she could pick up some wrapping paper when they went grocery shopping, since the children were anxious to wrap the gifts they'd purchased for their mother. By the time he came home, the gifts had been wrapped and supper was on the table. While they were eating bacon-potato soup with thick slices of French bread, Helen said, "The children were wanting to get Christmas decorations out. I noticed the boxes in Tamara's room marked 'Christmas,' and they were wondering if we could get them out tomorrow and get started."

She was relieved that he seemed pleased. "That would be fine," he agreed. "I'm certain they'd enjoy that. And thank you for getting the wrapping paper, and . . ." He motioned in the general direction of the wrapped gifts as he put food into his mouth.

"No problem," Helen said, trying to recall the last time she had enjoyed Christmas preparations this much. When she spent Christmas at home, she simply involved herself in her family's traditions. And the few

Christmases she'd spent on her own, she'd decorated and baked and purchased gifts for friends and family, but it had all been a very lonely, almost tedious string of occurrences leading up to an uneventful holiday. She loved Christmas and had a deep respect for the meaning of the holiday, but it was difficult to enjoy it fully without a family of her own to share it with. Her brothers had families of their own, and her parents were very much wrapped up in their grandchildren. So, whether she spent Christmas with them or on her own, it was still lonely.

But now she had Scotty and Tamara and their very busy, distracted father. She had realized more recently that even when he was home, he did a great deal of paperwork related to his job, and it was difficult for him to fit in extras with the children. She was only too glad to compensate, hoping in her heart that when Shayne Brynner got his miracle and his wife came home, she would still be able to spend some time with the children.

The next afternoon, once the homework and reading were finished, Helen got the Christmas boxes out and organized their contents with the children's help. She noticed that everything had been put away very haphazardly, and wondered what the situation might have been the previous Christmas.

Together they set out a nativity scene, hung the wreath on the door, and decorated the apartment with a number of holiday trinkets. They listened to some Christmas CDs they'd found, and sang along as they worked. Helen found an artificial tree that needed to be assembled, along with all of the lights and decorations to go on it. But she simply organized them and set them aside, thinking it would be more appropriate for the children to decorate the tree with their father.

The next day when she came, the tree had been set up and decorated, and the apartment had a cozy, festive feel to it. With only a week left until Christmas vacation, Helen asked Shayne if he would allow her to help the children get some gifts for him. At first he insisted that it wasn't necessary, but she tactfully assured him that the children needed to get something for their father. He agreed and provided her with some money, but Helen discussed a few ideas with the children and found they were excited at the prospect of making gifts for their father, so they went to purchase some materials instead.

With only one day left before school let out for Christmas, Tamara and Scotty had the gifts for their father wrapped and beneath the tree, and they were rolling out sugar cookies and cutting them into Christmas shapes. Helen was doing her best to just supervise and let them do it, despite knowing the mess would be much worse than if she did it herself. When the phone rang, she was the only one who didn't have cookie dough on her hands.

"Hello," she said.

"Who's this?" asked the voice on the other end. Helen knew it was Margie Brynner.

"This is the sitter. May I help you?"

"You must be Miss Star," she said as if she knew something scandalous.

"Yes, actually," Helen said with no tone of apology.

"You're all the children talk about," Margie said as if it were delightful, but her tone subtly implied that it wasn't. "Miss Star this. Miss Star that. You certainly seem to be having a good time with my children."

Helen bit her tongue to keep from saying that *somebody* had to. Instead she replied, "Would you like to talk to the children? They're rolling out cookies, but I can have them cleaned up in just a second." Not waiting for a response, she just set the receiver down, quickly wiped off Scotty's hands, and scooted him toward the phone.

"Hi Mom," he said with some enthusiasm. "We're making cookies, and we made paper chains to hang around the windows, and we made Christmas presents for Daddy, and—" He stopped and looked dismayed. The remainder of the conversation consisted of his usual one-word answers and grunting, then he handed the phone to Tamara, who had been washed up and was eagerly waiting to talk.

"Guess what, Mom!" she said as Scotty sulked off down the hall. "We got you presents and Miss Star took us to buy wrapping paper and we got some paper with sugarplum fairies on because you like sugarplum fairies and we wrapped your presents in it with pretty bows and they're under the Christmas tree so when you come home we can—" Now Tamara stopped. But she didn't look dismayed. She looked downright upset. "But . . . you said you were . . . gonna come home for Christmas and . . ." Following a long pause where she was apparently listening, she shouted into the phone, "I hate you! I hate you! I don't want you to come home!" Tamara then threw the phone down and ran into the other room, crying.

"That went well," Helen said to the empty room. She lifted the receiver to hang it up, then realized that

Margie was still on the other end. "Sorry," Helen said into the phone, "Tamara's gone to her room."

"I don't know why those children don't have any manners," Margie said, as if it were all Helen's fault.

Helen disregarded the statement and forced herself to speak courteously. "Did you want me to have Mr. Brynner call you?" she asked.

"No," Margie said tersely, "just tell him I won't be coming for Christmas. I'm certain he can manage to keep the children entertained, especially if he has you to help him."

Helen swallowed hard and cleared her throat as if it could clear away her sudden rise of anger. Is that what she thought—that Christmas was an event that forced a parent to reluctantly entertain his children? "I'll tell him," was all she said before she hung up the phone.

Helen took a moment to collect herself before she went down the hall and found Scotty sitting on his bed, staring at the floor, and Tamara sprawled on her bed, sobbing hysterically. That was the difference between boys and girls, she thought. But she knew the heartache was the same for both of them.

"Come here, Scotty," she said, gently taking his hand. "Let's have a little talk." They walked across the hall and sat on the edge of Tamara's bed, where Helen urged the little girl next to her. "Now," she said, "why all the sadness?"

Tamara readily volunteered, "Mommy promised she would be here for Christmas, and now she's not coming."

"Maybe she's too ill to travel," Helen suggested, even though she doubted that was the reason.

"She's not," Tamara insisted. "She used to say she was too sick to cook dinner or to read stories. But then she'd go shopping with her friends and stay out late."

Helen sighed. Even if Margie was sick now, the children would never believe it.

"Maybe she can't afford the flight home," Helen suggested.

"Grandma has lots of money. She paid for Mommy to go visit her lots of times."

So much for that theory, Helen thought. These kids were smart, and they obviously knew their mother well. And Helen was grateful now for the information Shayne had given her concerning the situation—information that had been glaringly validated in the last few minutes.

Helen uttered a silent prayer, wanting to say the right thing to help soothe the hurt these children were feeling. It occurred to her that nothing she could say would actually take the hurt away. It was more important to help them know where they stood in the midst of so much confusion.

"You know," Helen said, "sometimes it's hard to understand why grownups do the things they do. I don't know why your mother doesn't want to come home. But I *do* know, beyond any doubt, that her reasons have nothing to do with the two of you."

This statement piqued the children's interest, and Scotty's eyes especially showed unmasked hope. "You are both very good children," she said, "but even if you weren't, that wouldn't be the reason your mother left, or the reason she didn't come home. I'm certain that she loves you. It just seems that she needs to live with her mother, because that's where she's more comfortable."

"Because she's sick?" Tamara asked.

"I believe that's part of it. And the rest of it I don't understand, but . . ." Helen looked into their hopeful eyes and had to fight to hold back her own emotion. She had grown up in a home with two loving parents who loved each other. But through her teaching she had seen firsthand some of the heartache that came from a parent making bad choices and not being committed to marriage and children. It was tragic, plain and simple. "But," she finally swallowed her tears and finished, "it really doesn't matter why your mother does what she does. What matters is that you do your very best to be the kind of children your Heavenly Father wants you to be. Because He loves you no matter what. And you know what else? You're very lucky children, because you have a father who lives right here with you, and he loves you very much. He will always make sure that you're cared for and loved."

"And we have you," Tamara said.

"Yes," Helen said with a cracked voice, "and you have me."

"How come you're crying?" Scotty asked when she couldn't hold the tears back any longer.

"Because I'm very, very grateful that I have the two of you."

They both hugged her tightly, as if to reciprocate the feeling. Nothing more was said, but Helen felt that they had enough information to absorb for one day. Before she had a chance to dry her tears, she glanced up to see Shayne standing in the doorway. The children both rushed to his arms while Helen discreetly wiped a hand over her face.

"What's wrong?" he asked, more to Helen.

"Mommy's not coming home for Christmas," Tamara reported.

Shayne fought to contain the sudden rush of emotion that engulfed him. He'd been trying so hard to convince himself that she would come home for the holidays, and it would be a grand first step toward putting things right. He'd completely blocked out any thought that tempted him to believe she wouldn't be coming. But now it struck him between the eyes, and he knew he couldn't keep ignoring the reality. He had to break through the denial he'd buried himself in. He knew it in his heart. This was the beginning of the end.

Looking into his children's confused faces, he knew that now wasn't the time to express all he was feeling. He wondered what he could possibly say. His tongue felt frozen, and his head felt as if it weighed a hundred pounds. He glanced toward Helen, as if she might have the same comfort for him that she'd obviously been giving the children. He was more relieved than he could say when she answered his silent plea with her simple wisdom. "No matter what she chooses to do or not do, it doesn't change the love you have for each other, or the fact that your Heavenly Father loves all of you—and He will help you through whatever happens. It's Christmastime, and it's important to remember that Jesus was born, and lived, and died to take away the burdens of our sorrows. Everything will be all right."

Shayne nodded, unable to speak, consumed now with a different kind of emotion. The enormity of their past struggles, and the probability of more difficulties to come, suddenly seemed bearable in light of the perspective

Helen Starkey had just reminded him of. She truly was a light in the darkness, like some kind of angel sent from heaven to help guide them through this horrible pall.

"Everything will be all right," he echoed as he pulled the children close to him. "We have each other, and everything will be all right."

"And we have Miss Star," Tamara said with a hopeful note. "She'll be here for Christmas."

The mood suddenly changed as Helen met Shayne's eyes and it was evident that he shared her alarm. How could they explain to a six-year-old that it was inappropriate for Helen to spend Christmas with them under the circumstances?

She was relieved when Shayne spoke with a cautious expression in his eyes. "I'm certain Miss Star has other plans for the holiday." When the children looked dismayed, he added quickly, "I think Aunt Libby's coming for Christmas, and—"

"But Miss Star needs to come when we open presents, and—"

"I think we should talk about this tomorrow," Helen interrupted. "Right now, I need to clean up and go home. Twinkle is waiting for me." She hurried to the kitchen and quickly put the cookie dough in the fridge to be rolled out and baked the next day. She was just wiping off the flour-dusted countertop when Shayne appeared without the children.

"Thank you," he said with warmth in his voice. "I shudder to think where we would be now without you. I don't say it often enough, but your willingness to give has blessed our lives immensely, and I truly appreciate all you do."

"It's my pleasure, really," she admitted, afraid she might start crying again.

"I still feel like I should be paying you for your time, or at least give you some kind of compensation."

"Oh, no," she said, keeping her concentration on scraping the traces of cookie dough from the countertop. "That would somehow defeat the purpose for me. I'm only too glad to help. I've really grown to love Scotty and Tamara." She looked up at him and added, "They'll be all right, you know. They're stronger than you think."

Shayne wanted to tell her that he felt certain the children were a great deal stronger than he was, and perhaps that's what frightened him most. But he only nodded.

"Listen," she said as she rinsed out the dishrag in the sink, "we got making cookies, and we just didn't get anything cooked for supper or—"

"Don't worry about it," he said. "You cook too much as it is. Perhaps it's a good night to take them out to eat. Getting out might be good for all of us. I'd like to invite you to come along, but . . ." He hesitated, feeling suddenly awkward in his attempts to clarify his concerns.

"It's all right," she said. "I understand."

Helen quickly said good-bye to the children and hurried from the apartment, not certain why she was suddenly so overcome with emotion that she cried all the way home. Of course, she felt sadness and concern on behalf of the children—and their father. But there seemed to be something more, something that she couldn't quite put her finger on.

Helen pulled a leftover serving of chicken enchiladas from the freezer and heated it in the microwave while

she got into her pajamas and gave the cat some attention. She felt too drained to even do a load of laundry or
put her few dirty dishes into the dishwasher. Thoughts
of tomorrow depleted her further. The last day of school
before Christmas was always fun, but the children
would be hyper and difficult to keep in line.

While Twinkle rubbed her legs and meowed her
pleas for attention, Helen ate her supper and brushed
her teeth. Then she crawled into bed far earlier than
usual, suddenly feeling more lonely than she ever had in
her life.

⋰✳⋱

Shayne was surprised at how well he actually slept.
He'd cried his eyes out once he knew the children were
sleeping, then he'd slept dreamlessly and awakened early
enough to fix pancakes for breakfast before the usual
day began. His work seemed to drag as he contemplated
an idea that he hoped would help the children get
through the holiday more easily—and himself, too, he
had to admit.

He arrived home a little later than usual, since he'd
worked hard to get a little ahead in order to spend more
time with the children during the holiday break.
Entering the apartment, he was immediately aware of an
intangible comfort. The lights on the Christmas tree
twinkled. A Christmas hymn floated quietly from the
stereo. And a pleasant aroma drifted from a warm oven.
Helen was supervising the children at the kitchen table
while they frosted and decorated little sugar cookies. He
fussed over what they were doing and ate two cookies,

each one made especially for him with a ridiculous amount of little sprinkles piled on it. While Helen was stirring something on top of the stove, he spoke to her quietly. "Will you still be able to take the children during the days while—"

"Of course," she said. "I'm looking forward to it."

"You know," he said, "it's occurred to me that while you probably know far too much about me, I know practically nothing about you . . . at least in the sense of . . . well . . . What I'm trying to say is, *do* you have plans for Christmas? Surely you have family or—"

"Actually, my family lives in Idaho, and I won't be able to go home this year. But it's not the first time, and I'm okay with it. My parents are coming for a visit between Christmas and New Year's Day." She knew she was sounding more optimistic about the situation than she felt, but the last thing she wanted was to have him feeling sorry for her. Or worse, to have him know that the biggest reason she was staying here for Christmas was her lack of funds.

"Well," he said, "I was thinking . . . and tell me if I'm out of line here, or if you just don't want to, but . . . I know it wouldn't be appropriate for just you to be here for Christmas, but . . . Well . . ." He hesitated, and Helen realized he was nervous. She turned fully toward him and motioned for him to go on. "The thing is . . . my Aunt Libby is coming. She'll be here the day after tomorrow, and she's staying until the twenty-seventh. And with her here, I just don't see any reason why you can't at least be here with the children Christmas morning, and have supper with us on Christmas Eve. I really think it would help the children not feel their mother's absence so much. Think about it, and let me know if you—"

"I'd love to," she said, feeling more relief than she could possibly express. The thought of missing out on being with the children as they enjoyed their celebrations was downright depressing. She'd never met Aunt Libby, but she already considered her forthcoming visit a blessing, since she could now appropriately make the offer she'd been mulling around for days. "And perhaps Aunt Libby would be willing to join all of us at my house for dinner on Christmas Day. I love to cook, but . . . well . . . it doesn't mean much without someone to share it with. What do you say?"

He smiled. "I'm certain the children will be delighted."

Helen hurried to help the children clean up the cookie mess, and they sat to eat before she went home with a plate of cookies decorated with lots of love and sugar. The next few days went quickly as Helen had the children with her while Shayne worked. She watched them at her house so she could get her laundry and cleaning caught up and do some baking. In the hours without them, she did some last-minute Christmas shopping, visited Carla and took her a gift, and delivered goodies to friends and neighbors. Her mother called to say that they would be bringing gifts for Helen on their post-Christmas visit rather than sending them, since she was making something that wasn't quite finished.

The day before Christmas Eve, Shayne called to say that Aunt Libby had arrived and she would be caring for the children. Helen kept busy with some self-appointed projects and found she was greatly anticipating the holiday. She almost felt guilty for being a little glad that Margie Brynner had unwittingly given her the opportunity to spend Christmas with this sweet little family.

With her refrigerator well stocked and her Christmas dinner carefully planned, Helen made certain everything was in order before she went to the Brynners' apartment late in the afternoon on Christmas Eve, feeling a childlike excitement that she'd not felt since . . . surprisingly enough, since she was a child.

The air was especially cold and the sky was dark and gray, but Helen felt bright in her heart. Shayne answered the door, actually looking quite cheerful. But there was no disguising the ever-present sadness in his eyes, and she hoped he would eventually find a way to get beyond this struggle in his life. He was a good man, she thought, and he deserved to be happy.

"Come in," he said, motioning with his arm. "You must meet Aunt Libby. The children have told her so much about you, she swears she can't live another day without meeting you."

Helen chuckled softly just as the children came running to greet her with laughter and hugs. They both chattered excitedly at the same time as they led her into the kitchen, where Libby Brynner was busy at the stove. She turned with a big smile, wiping her hands on her full-length apron that read *Kiss the Cook*. Helen guessed her to be in her late fifties. She was a little taller than Helen, and much thinner. Her golden hair was streaked with hints of gray but styled in a way that made her seem younger. She was dressed in jeans and a sweatshirt, and her face nearly beamed in a way that made it evident this woman lived life to its fullest. Helen liked her before she even opened her mouth to say, "So this is Miss Star. It is indeed a pleasure."

"It's Miss Starkey, actually," she said, shaking the older woman's hand. "But you should call me Helen. And the pleasure is all mine."

"Aunt Libby's making crepes," Tamara said. "That's what they eat in France. Aunt Libby used to live in France."

"How exciting," Helen said.

"I went on a mission there, actually," Libby said as if it were nothing.

"One of her three missions," Shayne interjected.

"That's wonderful," Helen said. "Where else did you go?"

"Venezuela," she answered. "Twice."

While they ate crepes with a meat filling for supper, and crepes with strawberries and cream for dessert, Libby entertained them with stories from her missions, while the children asked question after question about the countries and the people. She talked of the different Christmas customs with a zeal that made it evident her missions had been great highlights in her life.

Through the remainder of the evening, as they read the Christmas story from the Bible and prepared for Santa's visit, Helen felt a deep admiration growing inside her for Aunt Libby. And it was evident that Shayne and his children felt the same way—but she suspected it was for different reasons.

Long after the children had gone reluctantly to bed, Libby regaled Shayne and Helen with stories of her life's experiences, including some that Shayne declared he'd heard many times but never tired of. Helen thoroughly enjoyed every minute, but the reasons didn't occur to her until she was in her own bed later that night. Libby Brynner was a sister to Shayne's father, and she had never married. The right opportunity had simply never presented itself, she'd said matter-of-factly. But it was plainly evident that Libby was happy. She had a fulfilling career that managed to support her adequately and fund her missions. She volunteered at homeless shelters, abuse shelters, and intensive care nurseries. She traveled regularly to maintain the relationships she shared with her many nieces and nephews, always on hand when she was needed most. She had spent count-less hours in family history libraries. Her genealogical work was one of her deepest loves.

As Helen lay in her bed, recounting all she had learned from Libby in one evening, she felt a new perspective fall over her—and with it came peace. Of course Helen would like to get married and have a family of her own. But Libby's example had made it evident that if the opportunity never came, it was entirely possible to be complete and fulfilled and to make an incredible difference in the world. In fact, Helen could see that Libby had been given many oppor-tunities to serve and share her talents that wouldn't have come to her if she had been married.

There hadn't been a moment since the Brynner family had come into her life that Helen had wondered about her purpose for being there for them at the right time. But she had never dreamed that acting on the opportunity to serve them would bring such a profound blessing into her life. She felt certain the insights Libby

Brynner had given her in one evening would give her strength and guidance through the remainder of her life. Helen wanted to be that kind of woman. She wanted to give and serve and live life to its fullest. And if the opportunity to marry and bear children never came to her in this life, she would still accomplish that quest— just as Libby had done.

Helen turned her thoughts to Scotty and Tamara. She imagined them sleeping peacefully in their little beds, with thoughts of Baby Jesus, and the anticipation of Santa's arrival filling their dreams. Feeling what she believed to be a similar combination of excitement and contentment, she drifted off to sleep.

Shayne had promised to call her the moment the children were awake, and the children had promised that they wouldn't open any presents until she got there. The phone rang at six-twenty, and Helen knocked on their apartment door at six thirty-seven. She'd purposely worn some pajamas that her brother had given her a few years back. They were flannel, with cats wearing red and green sweaters all over them. She called them "The Cat's Pajamas." And since they were ridiculously modest, she felt certain they'd be appropriate for the occasion. Shayne answered the door wearing sweats, and the children rushed to greet her with more energy than a nuclear power plant. Helen laughed out loud when she saw that Libby was wearing equally ridiculous pajamas. Then Libby laughed with her as the two of them dramatically imitated models on a runway before they settled down to enjoy the children's discovery of Christmas offerings. Helen was touched by the way Shayne had them kneel together for prayer before they began, then he required that a gift could not be opened without the receiver first telling something they were grateful for.

The excitement of the gift-opening frenzy was balanced with a gentle spirit of gratitude that kept the perspective of Christmas hovering close by. Helen was touched beyond words to open a beautiful journal from Libby. It was white and gold with a captivating picture of Christ on the front. "How did you know?" she asked.

"Know what?" Libby replied.

"That I'm a journal writer, and I'm always in need of a new one."

"Well, I figured if you weren't you ought to be," Libby said. "There must a great deal of value in the experiences you encounter in your work, my dear. Not to mention the things you must have learned from these two little rascals." Libby tousled Scotty and Tamara's hair, then drew them to her in a hug mingled with laughter.

Helen was surprised, and a little embarrassed, to open a number of lovely gifts. Shayne declared firmly that they were from the children, but she felt certain he had been involved in acquiring them. Children wouldn't have picked out a skirt and sweater set—in exactly her size. They also gave her a gift certificate from a kitchen specialty store in the mall, and a book. Helen reminded herself to be gracious, certain this was Shayne's way of expressing his gratitude when she had refused any payment. But she let them know how much she appreciated their thoughtfulness, and couldn't help thinking that it was nice to feel pampered by someone besides her parents.

The children were most excited about the gift they had for Twinkle: a toy mouse stuffed with catnip. "Well, you can give it to Twinkle yourself when you come over for Christmas dinner," she said. "And I've got some presents for all of you that you can open when you get there."

The children obviously liked that idea. Libby supervised cleaning up the mess of wrappings and packages, then the children played with their new things while Shayne insisted that the ladies sit and rest while he made pancakes in animal shapes.

Helen went home after breakfast and put the ham and scalloped potatoes in the oven before she lay down for a short nap. By the time the Brynner family arrived in mid-afternoon, she had the table set with a festive appeal that she couldn't help taking pride in.

The children were too excited about their gifts to possibly eat first. And Helen couldn't deny that she had similar feelings. They were as thrilled as she'd hoped they would be by the scrapbook binders she'd given them, including some pages featuring pictures of them with their mother. She'd found the photographs in a desk drawer in the apartment and had asked Shayne privately if she could use them for this purpose. "A scrapbook is to help you remember things in your life that can cheer you up when you're feeling sad," she pointed out. "No matter what happens with your mom, you can look at your books and know that you'll always have your memories of being together, and she will always be your mom."

"Thank you, Helen," Tamara said, giving her a tight hug. Then Scotty did the same, and Helen felt a tingle of warmth rush through her. Their joy increased when they each opened more scrapbook supplies, and a plastic box brightly decorated with stickers to keep their supplies in, as well as to store items that would eventually go into the book. Helen promised to help them put the pages together whenever they wanted to work on them.

Helen gave Libby a gift set with bath things and a candle, all with the fragrance of rose and prettily packaged in a basket.

"Oh, I love smelly things," Libby declared, and took out each item to sniff it and let the children do the same.

Helen gave Shayne a recipe box with little wooden stars glued all over it. He laughed when he saw it, commenting on the decor of her own kitchen. But he especially loved the recipe cards inside with simple recipes written on them, and all of the ingredients needed listed on the back.

"That's just for weekends and emergencies," she said. "Until Margie comes back, I still intend to do the cooking during the week."

She also gave him a silly apron that he declared would give Libby a run for her money. He put it on to help her in the kitchen a few minutes, then they all sat down to a fine meal. When they were nearly finished eating, Helen mentioned, "I bought everything to make fruitcake several days ago, and I just haven't gotten around to it. I was hoping to share it with you, but I guess it will have to wait."

"Fruitcake?" Shayne laughed. "I must confess I've never tasted a fruitcake I liked. It doesn't have a very good reputation, you know."

"I know," Helen said. "But *my* fruitcake is different. It's my mother's recipe. It's moist and delicious, and you'll love it. I promise. For me, it just doesn't seem like Christmas without it. Next year, I'll have to be more on the ball."

"Well, I hope I don't have to wait that long to taste it," Shayne said. "Now you've got me curious."

The time went too quickly as they visited and the children played with some of their new toys they had brought with them. It became evident that Scotty and Tamara were tired when they began whining and bickering, and Shayne insisted they needed to get home and catch up on all the sleep they didn't get the night before.

"What are you doing tomorrow?" Libby asked, and Helen wondered if she had sensed Helen's disappointment at having to say good-bye.

"Nothing, really . . . unless Shayne wants me to watch the children, of course. But I assumed with you being here . . ."

"Well, I was planning on being with them," Libby said, "but I wondered if you would come and keep me company, since I promised them they could play at McDonald's. We can have lunch and . . . Let me put it this way: I'd much rather while away the time with you than read."

"I'd love to," Helen said.

"Good." Libby put on her coat. "We'll pick you up at eleven-thirty."

"I'll be ready."

"Thank you, Helen," Shayne said while Libby was herding the children toward the door. "It's been a wonderful holiday—and having you be a part of it certainly made a difference. Being here is . . . well, it reminds me somehow of Christmas when I was a kid. I can't explain it, really. It just does."

Helen smiled. "Thanks for letting me share it with you and the children." She laughed softly. "And I love Libby."

"How can you not?" He hurried out the door, calling back to say, "Merry Christmas, Helen."

"Same to you," she called and watched them drive away.

Helen let out a lonely sigh in their absence. But Twinkle rubbed up against her legs, as if to remind her that she would always have company. And Helen couldn't deny what a wonderful holiday it had been. She felt truly blessed.

In spite of her nap, Helen went to bed early and slept well. The following morning, she had just enough time to shower and put in a load of laundry before it was time to go with Libby and the children.

While Scotty and Tamara played to their hearts' content, Helen enjoyed hearing more about Libby's life, again marveling at her incredible attitude and vibrant spirit. Helen was momentarily surprised when Libby began asking her extensive questions about her life, but they were soon talking comfortably as if they'd known each other forever.

When the conversation began to wind down and Scotty and Tamara had explored the play area sufficiently, Helen took the opportunity to share her sentiment while the children were putting on their shoes. "I want to thank you, Libby," she said. "I must admit that your example has helped my perspective immensely. It's not that I haven't been happy. It's just that you've helped me see the potential of all that I *can* do with my life. I wish every single woman could have someone like you to look up to."

"Oh, you're too sweet," Libby said, giving Helen a quick hug. "The thing is, I know that I'll get the blessings I earn in this life. *All* of them. I just have to work for it. And I'm certain there's some wonderful young man—who was killed in one of the great wars—just waiting on the other side to make me his wife. With him, I will share every blessing in eternity that comes from being faithful and doing the best I could with what I had to work with."

The thought struck Helen so deeply that she actually got tears in her eyes. She marveled freshly at the love and respect she felt for this woman she had known so briefly, and she dreaded having her leave town tomorrow. But she was able to spend a little more time with her as they visited through the afternoon, and they exchanged addresses and phone numbers, promising to keep in touch.

BACON-POTATO SOUP

1 package sliced bacon, cut in small pieces
8 to 10 medium potatoes, peeled and cut
in small pieces
2 cups cheese, shredded
Chopped onion, salt, and pepper to taste

Fry bacon pieces until crisp. Drain grease and set bacon aside. Cook potatoes and onions in enough water to cover them, in the same pan so the bacon flavor cooks into the broth. When potatoes are tender, add thickening, cheese, bacon, salt and pepper.

Thickening: *1/2 cup flour and 1 cup water*

Mix and add slowly while stirring.
If you want the soup thicker, add more.

Chapter 5

Helen stayed in bed late on the morning of the twenty-seventh. She knew that Libby would be leaving this morning, but they'd already said their good-byes and promised to keep in touch. Shayne would be going into work late in order to see Libby off, so Helen took her time with showering and having breakfast. She called Carla to verify their plans of taking the children to Peter Piper Pizza for lunch, then she went to the apartment to take over so Shayne could get to work by eleven.

Helen knocked at the door, but there was no response. She glanced around to verify that Shayne's truck was there, then she knocked again. She wondered if there had been some delay in Libby's departure, and perhaps they'd gone somewhere together in her car. Knowing he always locked the door when he went out, she carefully tried the knob, and was surprised to feel it turn in her hand. Wondering if they were just busy in one of the back rooms, she carefully pushed the door open just a few inches. She let out a little gasp to see Shayne seated on the couch, his head in his hands. Feeling that she'd invaded his privacy, she hurried to close the door just as he lifted his head to see her.

"Forgive me," she said. "I just assumed that—"

"It's all right," he said in a voice that was strained and raspy. "I should have answered the door. I just didn't have . . . the strength."

Helen's heartbeat quickened as she realized that something was terribly wrong. She wasn't certain what to do, but she voiced her first thought. "Are the children—"

"They'd been asking to go next door and play. I needed some time alone, so I told them I'd call when you got here."

"If you'd like I could get them and be off so you can be alone and . . ." Her words faded as he looked at her deeply and tears streamed down his face. He said nothing, but she knew there was something he needed to say. Treading carefully, she said, "If it's none of my business, just say so, but if there's something I can do . . ."

He wiped his hand over his face, seeming embarrassed and distraught. Helen closed the door and leaned against it. "What's happened?" she asked, at the risk of being nosy.

Shayne nodded toward some papers lying beside him on the couch. "I don't know how to tell the children," he said. He motioned toward them with his hand, and Helen took it as permission to look and see what they were. She picked them up as if they might burn her hands, and it only took a moment for her to understand. *Divorce papers.*

"When did you—"

"Libby hadn't been gone ten minutes when they were delivered. I knew what it was before I opened it, so I sent the children next door."

"I can't believe it," Helen said, realizing that she had become more emotionally involved than she wanted to admit. In her heart she had truly believed that a miracle would happen, and Margie Brynner would come home to the husband and children who loved her. She felt a degree of shock settle in, yet she couldn't begin to understand what Shayne was feeling right now. She thought of the children and their hopes for their mother's return, and she felt sick to her stomach.

"That's what I said," Shayne replied, startling her from her thoughts.

"Did you have any indication that she would take it this far? Has she talked to you about this?"

"Not a word," he said. "She's been hesitant to come home, even reluctant to talk to me beyond necessary trivialities. But I never dreamed it would come to this without some kind of . . . warning." His voice cracked with that last word, and Helen resisted the urge to reach out and put her arms around him like she would have one of the children.

"I know things have been rough," he went on. "I know we've disagreed on many things. But I always did what I felt was best . . . for all of us. I never wanted *this!* Divorce is such an ugly thing. It's not what I wanted . . . for me . . . for the children. And for Margie."

"Have you talked to her?"

"I called her just before you came."

"And?" Helen pressed when he hesitated.

"Her mother told me she didn't want to talk to me, and whatever I needed could be handled through her attorney."

Helen sucked in her breath as if she could perceive the literal amputation Shayne must be feeling to have his wife cut off from him so completely.

"And then . . ." Shayne went on and his voice broke, "her mother said . . ." He cleared his throat and seemed to push the words out with a burst of courage. "'Why can't you just accept that you're not capable of taking care of her?'" He coughed as if to fight off his growing emotion. "I wanted to tell her that I knew Margie was capable of taking care of herself, but I knew it wouldn't make any difference. And I would have just made a fool of myself by blubbering all over the place. If Margie's health was so poor that she was confined to bed for the rest of her life, I would have done my best to care for her and make the most of it. It is possible to be a good wife and mother, even if you're bedridden. But she wanted no interaction with me or the children at all. She was too ill to be a wife and mother, but not too ill to go shopping with her friends. I've tried every avenue I could possibly come up with to solve the problems effectively. I don't know what else I can do. I've thought it through over and over in the months since she left, wondering if I could have done something differently. I'm certainly not perfect, and I've made my mistakes, but everything I did I felt I had to do. I felt it was right. I just never dreamed . . . it would come to this."

When he said nothing more, Helen glanced quickly through the papers in her hands, as if they could answer the question that had just struck fear into her heart. When she couldn't find the answer amidst all the legal jargon, she just murmured, "Please don't tell me she wants the children. After the way she ran off, she can't possibly intend to—"

"Oh, no," he said with the first measure of peace she'd heard in his voice since she'd arrived. "It's very clear that I have full physical custody. She's entitled to an occasional visit. That's all she wants, apparently."

Helen sighed so deeply that she nearly lost her breath. "Well, that certainly is a blessing," she said. "I would hate to see the children dragged through custody battles."

"Yes," he said firmly, "that is a blessing, except . . . I wonder how the children will perceive this. Will it appear to them that their mother doesn't want them?"

"Well, she doesn't, now does she?"

"No, but . . . how will that make them feel?"

"I'm certain it will be difficult, but then, they've been getting that message in one way or another for a very long time."

"That's true," Shayne said, then he became distant again.

"What about other stipulations?" she asked at the risk of being insensitive. But she felt she had to know, if only to have the information she needed to help the children adjust.

"There are no stipulations," he said. "She's not asking for any alimony—or anything. But then, I'm certain she knows that if she did, I could very quickly produce evidence of the vast amounts of money she spent, forcing me to sell the house in order to pay off her debts. I've got a deep stack of credit card receipts with her signature on them from purchases that couldn't possibly be of any benefit to the family. Expensive meals, expensive clothes, gifts for her friends. You name it."

He fell silent again, and Helen felt a sudden rush of compassion for him that moved her to tears. He looked so helpless, so hopeless. She uttered a silent prayer that she might be able to find words to give him the strength and direction he needed. His parents were on a mission. His aunt was on her way home and couldn't even be reached by phone for many hours yet. Did he have any friends? None that she'd seen evidence of. But whether or not he did, she was here now. And now was the moment that he needed to know he could make it through another day.

"Shayne," she said as an idea settled comfortably into her mind. He looked up with a hope in his eyes that touched her. Did he have so much faith in her to give him the advice he needed? She cleared her throat quietly and continued. "I can't possibly say that I know how you feel. I can try to understand, but in truth, I can't. I know that from where you are now, the future seems difficult and uncertain. But I do know you can make it through this. As I see it, your wife separated herself from you and the children a long time ago. Divorce is a terrible thing, but in many cases, it's better than any other option if a person chooses to behave badly and not be committed to making a marriage work. In this case, maybe divorce is a blessing. Perhaps it's good that at least Margie is willing to admit that she's not committed to being a wife and mother, and she's willing to let go, rather than leaving you and the children hanging in this horrible limbo, not knowing what to expect from one day to the next. Now you can press forward and build a new life for your children, knowing that you're not hanging on to some obscure hope that will never be realized. Better this than being forced yourself to carry out divorce proceedings because she refused to be a part of your family."

Her words suddenly ran out, but she sensed him absorbing them and allowed him the silence to do so. When he turned to look at her as if to say that he understood—at least to some degree—she felt pleased to see a measure of hope in his eyes that had replaced the fear and despair. Instinctively she took his hand and squeezed it, hoping he understood the full depth of her concern for him and his children. He squeezed back and glanced at their clasped hands, then back to her face. As their eyes met, she felt something shift inside her at the same moment his expression seemed to subtly imply a hidden message. Helen didn't understand why her heart began to pound and her stomach fluttered, but she abruptly withdrew her hand, feeling suddenly frightened without understanding why. He looked briefly alarmed but she chuckled tensely, and forced a smile.

"Forgive me," she said, "I'm certain I've stepped beyond my bounds."

"On the contrary," he responded. "You've been a very good friend, and I don't know what I would have done without you."

Helen nodded, wondering how she could tell him that her opportunity to be involved with his family had made her life so rich. She simply said, "Like I've told you before, it's been my pleasure."

"Why is that?" he asked, and she wondered why the conversation had suddenly turned so dramatically toward her.

"Because I've grown to love Scotty and Tamara. They are very dear to me. It's not that I wasn't happy before, but . . . well, they've given my life something that was missing. That's all. And forgive me if I sound selfish, but . . .

well, I was worried that when Margie came back, she wouldn't want my help with the children. At least this way, I can remain involved and still . . . unless there's a reason you don't want me to be," she added as an after-thought.

"Oh, the children need you, Helen," he said. "Now, more than ever. And so do I . . . to help with the children, I mean."

"Of course," she said and stood abruptly, glancing at her watch. "Perhaps I should go get them now; we're meeting a friend and her children for lunch. And I'm certain you could use some time to yourself. Will you be going to work?"

"No, I already called and told them I couldn't make it. But I think you're right. I could use some time . . . to think."

Helen headed toward the door and he added, "I don't want to tell the children yet. I need a little more time to come to terms with it myself, and . . . I do need to talk to Margie . . . just to be absolutely certain there are no other options."

"I understand," she said, not daring to look at him for fear of having another reaction like the one she'd just recovered from.

"Helen," he said in a gentle voice just as she reached for the doorknob. When he said nothing more, she was forced to look up. He actually smiled, and sure enough, something stirred inside of her that she didn't under-stand and didn't want to acknowledge. "Thank you," was all he said. She nodded and hurried next door to collect Tamara and Scotty so they could be on their way.

Helen immersed herself in the chatter of the children as she drove to Peter Piper Pizza. She found Carla there, reading a book, and she quickly got the children some tokens and set them free to play with Carla's children on the numerous toys and arcades.

"I already ordered the pizza," Carla announced as Helen sat across from her. "I know what you like."

"Thank you," Helen said. "How much do I owe you?"

"Three hundred dollars," Carla said, then she laughed. "No, just give me a ten. That's close enough."

Helen dug into her purse for a ten-dollar bill and wondered why her hands were shaking.

"Is something wrong?" Carla asked, and for once Helen didn't appreciate her friend's perceptive nature.

"Yes, something's wrong," she said. "I just don't know why it's affecting me so personally."

"You're going to have to be a little more specific. As much as I'd like to read your mind, it's just not within the realms of my calling in life."

"Shayne was served with divorce papers this morning."

"Good heavens," Carla said breathlessly. "Do the children know?"

"No, he wants to come to terms with it a little more himself before he tells them. I think that's wise. But no matter how you look at it, this is going to be hard for all of them. I mean, from the children's perspective, even a bad mother is better than no mother at all. It seems she wants nothing more than an occasional visit. Of course, that's good because there won't be any custody battle, and Shayne will get to keep the children. They can stay where they're loved and secure. But still . . ." Her words faded with her thoughts.

"Yeah, I see what you mean." Carla turned toward Scotty and Tamara where they were playing with her own children. "It's heartbreaking."

"It makes me sick to my stomach," Helen said. "When I would give so much to have children of my own, to see a woman who cares so little for them, it's just so . . ." She checked herself when she heard the rising anger in her voice, then cleared her throat and added, "Of course, I don't know Margie Brynner, and I can't judge the full spectrum of what's taking place. There's plenty of evidence that she's selfish and uncommitted, but I don't know how she was raised, or where the desires of her heart are."

"Yeah," Carla said, "but no matter what *her* problems are, that still leaves a man and his children without her. And it's sad. I'm glad they have you."

"So am I," Helen said. "And I'm glad I have them."

Helen wanted to tell Carla that there was something else nagging at her; something that felt incredibly disconcerting. But she couldn't even put together in her mind what it was, so how could she possibly explain it to Carla? The feeling had started when she'd taken Shayne's hand, then he'd turned to look at her and . . . "Good heavens," Helen murmured before she had a chance to check herself.

"What?" Carla demanded.

"Oh, nothing," she insisted, too startled by the thought to even dare admit it aloud.

"You're lying. Something's bothering you. I can tell. Out with it."

Helen managed to change the subject, convincing Carla that her anxiety was nothing more than concern about the divorce and its effect on the children. She also managed to avoid seeing Shayne when she took the children home. But that night as she lay in bed, staring at the ceiling, she couldn't erase him from her mind. Something had changed in that moment when she'd taken his hand and he'd looked into her eyes. And that something was frightening—delightfully, wonderfully, splendidly frightening. The thought of feeling something beyond friendship for Shayne Brynner seemed foreign and outlandish. She told herself it was nothing more than a childish fantasy. She loved the children and wanted to be a part of their lives. Knowing he would soon be divorced, she'd simply indulged in a senseless, ridiculous fantasy for a fleeting moment. It had taken her off guard, and now she had to adjust her thinking and get beyond it. But when she woke up the next morning, her first thought was the memory of Shayne Brynner's smile. He called while she was fixing herself some toast, and just the sound of his voice made her stomach quiver. *He's still married,* she reminded herself. And even if he wasn't, she had no reason to believe that he would ever see anything more in her than his nanny-slash-housekeeper.

"Will you still be able to take the children today?" he asked.

"Of course. I'm looking forward to it."

"Great, but . . . Scotty said your parents are coming today."

"That's right. But's it's not a problem."

"If you're sure."

"Of course I'm sure," she insisted.

"Okay, well, thank you." He hesitated, and she

figured this would be an appropriate time to say good-bye, but he cleared his throat and she knew he wanted to say something else. "I was thinking," he began. "I haven't told the children yet, and . . . I was hoping you would be there when I do. You're not so emotionally involved, and . . . you have a way of saying things that help. I know I'm asking a lot, and I feel certain that you should feel like you're taken for granted, or at least taken advantage of . . . because you do so much, but . . . I'll even bribe you. What can I do for you, Helen?"

Get out of my head, she thought. "Just let me spend time with your children," she said.

"I'm already doing that, and I'm certain it's more of a blessing to me than it is you."

"It's all in how you look at it, I suppose."

"Well, I'll think of a way to repay you . . . eventually."

"I don't want you to—"

"Helen," he interrupted, "will you help me tell them?"

"Of course. When?"

"Well, I'm not certain, really. I'm not sure I'm ready yet, but . . . how long will your parents be here?"

"Just two nights."

"Well, after they go. We'll talk about it then."

"Okay," Helen said, wanting to get off the phone for reasons she refused to even think about.

"I'll drop the kids off in a little while."

"I'll be here," she said and gratefully ended the call. She immediately dialed Carla.

"Hey, what's up?" Carla asked.

"Something's wrong with me."

"It's that obsession you have with stars," Carla said.

"Which is so much worse than your obsession with cows," Helen said with sarcasm. "Now be serious."

"Okay. What is it? Is it the same thing you were trying to hide from me yesterday while you were shoving pizza in your face?"

"Yes, I suppose it is."

"I knew you were lying to me."

"Not lying," Helen said, "just . . . needing some time to be certain that it really was enough of a problem to talk about."

"Okay. Get to it already."

Helen took a deep breath. "I'm attracted to him."

Carla let out a loud one-syllable laugh. "That's it? That's a problem?"

"He's married, Carla."

"For another month, maybe."

"But I can't be feeling this way about a married man. It's wrong."

"If he were going to stay married, then I would say you're going to have to get a grip and get over it. But he's very nearly divorced."

"Very nearly isn't divorced enough. I shouldn't be feeling this way."

"Listen, sweetie," Carla said firmly, "a feeling is a feeling. It's not a sin. What you do with those feelings is a different matter, but as long as you're not getting romantic with him until the divorce is final, then what you feel is just that. It's what you feel."

Helen thought about that for a moment. "I hadn't looked at it that way." But then an even more frightening thought occurred to her. "Maybe he doesn't feel the same way about me."

"He's not divorced yet."

"Okay, but . . . maybe he never will feel the same way about me."

"Well, that's just something time will tell."

"I suppose," Helen said, feeling as if she'd just stepped off an ocean liner into a foreign country. She couldn't remember the last time she'd even gone out on a date, let alone had to contemplate such feelings.

"So, what else are you thinking?" Carla asked. "I know you're thinking something. Don't lie to me like you did yesterday. Just tell me."

"I didn't lie, but . . . well . . . I can't helping being . . . afraid."

"Of?" Carla drew out the word dramatically.

"Of . . . having him not find me attractive . . . ever. I mean . . . you said it yourself once. He's adorable. And I'm . . ."

"What? You're adorable, too."

"I suppose that's a matter of opinion, but . . . it's been years since I've tried to make myself attractive to a man. I don't know where to begin."

"You can begin by not trying at all. If he isn't attracted to you the way you are, if you have to change to get him to notice you, then he's not worth it."

"I can agree with that theory, but . . ."

"But?" Carla pressed.

Helen wanted to admit she was concerned that he might think her extra weight was a problem. But Carla struggled with superfluous pounds herself, and Helen didn't want to sound insensitive. Of course, Carla's husband had never let the weight Carla had gained with child-bearing and maturity bother him. He'd made it clear he loved her no matter what. And Helen wanted a man who felt the same way. Still, she couldn't help wondering if it was something that would bother Shayne Brynner.

"Nothing," Helen insisted. "I just need some time to think. Oh," she glanced at the clock, "speaking of which, he'll be here any minute with the kids, and I'm still in my pajamas."

Carla chuckled. "Bye. Call me later."

Shayne dropped the children off without coming in, which suited her just fine. The less she saw of him, the less likely she was to let this birdbrained whimsy get hold of her.

Helen anticipated her parents' arrival with childlike excitement. And they didn't disappoint her. Fred and Sadie Starkey were good, fun-loving people, and they arrived with arm-loads of packages and lots of laughter. Helen couldn't help feeling loved as she observed their obvious pleasure in being with her, and they took to the children with no difficulty whatsoever. They'd only been there an hour before Fred had them involved in a guessing game that he had often played with Helen when she was a child.

When Sadie announced that it was time for Helen to open her gifts, it became evident that they had also brought gifts for Scotty and Tamara. The children were delighted, and seemed oblivious to what Helen knew: not much money had been spent, but Fred and Sadie seemed to know the simple things that children enjoyed. While they sat at the counter with their new Play-Doh, Helen exchanged Christmas gifts with her parents. She was not surprised, but thoroughly pleased with the new afghan her mother had made. It was in dark green and burgundy, which went beautifully with the simple decor of Helen's family room. They were thrilled with Helen's gifts for them, which were mostly books. And she was equally delighted with the several little gifts they gave her—things that weren't expensive, but made her feel loved and pampered, from the new kitchen towels, to the scented bubble bath and candle.

Fred and Sadie played a board game with the children while Helen fixed an easy supper. Shayne came by earlier than she'd expected, and she hated the way her stomach was overrun with butterflies. She hoped he would quickly be off, but her parents kept visiting with him, and it would have been ridiculous for her not to invite him to eat with them. Helen attempted to keep her thoughts focused on the children, but she couldn't ignore the effect of Shayne's presence.

When he finally left with the children, Helen was assaulted with questions from her parents. She added a few more details to what she had already told them during previous phone conversations.

"Do you think they'll get back together?" Sadie asked, her brow furrowed with concern.

"No," Helen said. "He's been served with divorce papers." She couldn't help noticing a strong glance pass between her parents, and she wondered what they were thinking. "I kept hoping they would be able to work it out," she added, but it's become evident that his wife won't be coming back." She felt almost guilty as she said it, in light of her changing feelings. She quickly reminded herself that what she felt was nothing more than a passing fancy. She was happy. Her life was good, and she was determined to make the most of it. She didn't need a husband to do that!

"Helen?" her father said, startling her. "Where were you?"

"Oh . . . nothing. Just . . . thinking. Did you say something to me?"

"I said," Fred went on with a subtle smirk toward his wife, "he seems like a very nice man."

"And he's about your age, isn't he?" Sadie asked.

"He's younger, actually," Helen said as it became evident where this was headed. "But don't get any brilliant ideas. Yes, he is a nice man, and I've grown to love the children. But that doesn't mean that . . ."

"That what?" Sadie asked.

"Nothing," she said, moving toward the kitchen. "I just don't want you to be doing any matchmaking around here. Even *if* such a thing were feasible, he's still not even divorced."

Nothing more was said, but Helen feared that her vehement defensiveness had said far more about her feelings than if she had remained indifferent. But how could she be indifferent when she felt this way inside?

That night as she lay in bed, Helen vacillated back and forth between fantasies of marrying Shayne Brynner and living happily ever after, and the more likely reality of living out her life as a single woman with a great deal to give to the world. She felt certain that any hope she might have for a relationship with Shayne would simply be dashed. It was better that she remain rooted in reality—at least until she had some indication that such a relationship might be possible. But she had no reason to believe that such an attractive, successful man would ever fall in love with her. She forced her thoughts to Aunt Libby, certain that her influence was the biggest reason she had been led to these people. She finally fell asleep imagining herself becoming such a woman.

The following day, Helen enjoyed her visit with her parents as long as the conversation stayed clean away from Shayne Brynner. And her parents thoroughly enjoyed the children. That evening, while Sadie was helping Helen prepare vegetables for a relish tray, Tamara ran into the kitchen to get a drink of water. As soon as she'd gulped it down, she said to Helen, "It's almost New Year's. Are you going to come for New Year's like you did for Christmas? Are you, huh?"

Helen could almost literally feel herself turning warm, as if her attraction to Shayne Brynner somehow made Tamara's innocent suggestion a scandalous proposition. "I don't know, honey," she said, grateful that Tamara was too innocent to perceive her discomfort. But as the child scurried away, Helen looked up to see her mother's penetrating gaze. It was evident that Sadie Starkey could see right through her daughter's attempts to keep her feelings from showing.

"I think there's something you're not telling me," Sadie said.

Helen cleared her throat and returned to her work on the cutting board with extra vigor. "I don't know what you're talking about."

Sadie made a dubious grunt, then broke a stilted silence by adding, "You like him, don't you?"

"Who?" Helen asked, pretending to be inane.

"Give it up, girl," her mother said with a sideways smile. "I know you better than that. You become as flustered as a cat in a dog pound whenever he comes up. So what's the truth of it?"

Helen sighed and put down the knife. "Okay, fine. I admit that since it became evident he was getting divorced, my feelings have . . . changed. But that doesn't mean a thing. He's still married. And even if he weren't, I have no reason to believe that I could ever mean anything to him whatsoever."

"He seems like a wonderful man," Sadie said in a gentle voice that made Helen sigh.

"Yes, he is," Helen said, wishing it hadn't sounded so dreamy. "But . . ."

"But?" Sadie questioned.

"He's still married, and . . ."

"Okay, he's still married. But that doesn't mean you have to stuff your feelings in a hole. You should keep them to yourself, yes. But the divorce will happen, and then you can . . ."

"What?" Helen demanded, feeling as if her mother already had some easy little fairy-tale ending all worked out.

"Well . . . then you can see if there's anything to these feelings or not. Give it some time. Whatever is best will come together."

Helen nodded, certain her mother was right. But she didn't want to admit to the deeper feelings that were troubling her.

"What else?" Sadie asked right on cue, making it increasingly evident to Helen that there was no hiding her feelings from her mother.

Again Helen sighed, figuring she should just get her feelings into the open. In truth, she couldn't deny finding this a welcome opportunity. She respected her mother's wisdom, and perhaps she could help her sort out the confusion that was plaguing her.

"The thing is, Mom," she admitted, "even if by some remote possibility Shayne Brynner ever saw me as something more than a nanny and a good cook, I'm not certain I want to get married."

Following an astonished silence, Sadie forced her mouth to close and cleared her throat. "Excuse me while I go clean the wax out of my ears. I could have sworn you just said that you didn't want to get married."

"Oh, don't be flippant," Helen said.

"Who's being flippant?" Sadie retorted. "If you're afraid of getting your hopes up, fine. Just admit it and deal with it. But don't go convincing yourself that you don't *want* to get married. I know you better than that."

Helen sighed, wondering how to explain. "It's just that . . . I've spent a lot of years trying to become comfortable with being single. I'll admit that something was missing, but it's like I told you about Libby. Her example has made a huge difference. I feel like I've finally really come to terms with being single—just in the last few days. I've accepted it. I'm happy. I'm looking forward to all the things I can do with my life, and I can do it just the way I am."

Helen watched her mother's contemplative expression and expected some kind of argument or lecture. After a minute Sadie finally said, "Have you watched *The Sound of Music* lately?"

"No, why?" Helen couldn't see what that had to do with anything.

"Never mind. Just rent the video and watch it. And in the meantime, I want you to remember one thing.

Your Father in Heaven knows what's best for you, Helen. He knows the paths that your life is supposed to take. Whatever you do, don't let your own fears and concerns keep you from feeling the truth of His plan for you. You know how to go about making choices properly. You'll know what to do."

As Sadie turned her attention back to daintily arranging vegetables on a tray with some pickles and olives, Helen felt almost disappointed. She had perhaps been hoping to have her mother convince her of what she should do. But Sadie was obviously leaving it completely on Helen's shoulders—which was where it should be. Still, Helen felt a little unsettled. Then she reminded herself that Shayne Brynner was still a married man, and she doubted he would ever give her a second glance. So why was she so concerned about the whole thing, anyway?

Forcing her mind from memories of that smile that had the ability to make her insides turn to melting butter, Helen helped her mother put supper on the table.

"Cool," Scotty said as he was seated and Helen started dishing up his portion of meatballs. "It's those porcupine things."

"Oh, I love porcupines!" Tamara exclaimed.

"So do I," Fred agreed. "Helen learned to make them from Sadie. And Sadie's porcupine meatballs are one of my favorites."

A blessing was offered, and they began to eat in comfortable silence. As much as Helen tried to avoid such thoughts, she couldn't help contemplating how wonderful it would be if her parents could officially become Scotty and Tamara's grandparents. But again she had to remind herself that there was nothing to base any such idea upon. Scolding herself for letting her imagination run away with her, she recalled her mother's advice and felt certain Sadie had more insight than Helen wanted to admit. Maybe she was just afraid of getting her hopes up.

After supper, her parents took the children to rent some videos while Helen cleaned up the kitchen, contemplating the emotions that were surfacing in her. Her mother's words began to sink in, and she wondered if there was more to her fears than she was willing to admit.

Shayne stopped by to get the children while they were gone, and she did her best to appear indifferent and calm in his presence—just as she had always been before these ridiculous notions had gotten into her head.

"Listen," she said, "since the kids went to rent videos, I'm certain they'll be wanting to watch one. Would it be all right if they stay up late, since there's no school tomorrow?"

"That should be fine," he said, "unless you're tired of them, and—"

"Oh, no" she said, "that's not possible."

"But with your parents here . . ."

"They're enjoying Scotty and Tamara. They're all getting along just fine." She swallowed and forced herself to say, "You're welcome to join us." Inwardly she wondered how she would handle being in the same room with him all evening, while her parents would likely be sizing him up to see if they might go well together.

"Thank you," he said, "but . . . I've got some paper-work I need to get done before morning. If you'll just call me when you're finished, I can come and get them, and—"

"If it's all right with you," she added quickly, grateful he would be leaving soon, "why don't they just stay the night. They have toothbrushes here, and they can sleep in some of my T-shirts. Then you won't have to bring them back early."

"That sounds great," he said, "if you're sure."

"Of course. I wouldn't have asked if it would be a problem. They're great kids." *They have a great father,* she added to herself, and sighed loudly as she forced herself to look elsewhere.

"Have you eaten?" she asked, then quickly offered, "Let me fix you a plate to take home." At least that would prevent him from staying any longer.

"Thank you," he said. "I won't turn that down."

Helen quickly gathered some fresh vegetables into a little Zip-Loc bag, and she dished up a healthy serving of meatballs into a container that she could get later. She drew a deep breath of relief when he finally left, but she barely had time to collect herself before her parents returned.

Helen was actually relieved when they came home with *The Sound of Music* among their video selections. The children were excited that they would get to stay the night, and they all settled in the family room to watch the movie that Sadie had suggested would hold the answer to Helen's dilemma. It all became very clear when Maria was torn between her desire to be a nun and the love she felt for the Captain. The Mother

Superior summed it all up neatly when she told Maria that love between a man and a woman was a wonderful thing, and Maria chose the Captain. Helen told herself that she shouldn't expect such a fairy-tale ending in her own life, then she remembered that the movie had been based on actual events.

That night, as Helen lay in bed staring toward the window, she knew in her heart the course she needed to take. If marriage with Shayne became a possibility, and she came to know that it was right, she would take it on and live life to its fullest. And if it didn't work out, she would do the same. She would press forward with Libby's example in her heart. She drifted to sleep with thoughts of Shayne Brynner consuming her. She couldn't help hoping that somehow he was feeling the same way about her. But it just seemed too wonderful to be possible.

Fred and Sadie left the day before New Year's Eve, since they had a party at home with their family home evening group of retired couples. Helen couldn't help crying a little after they had gone. Their leaving reminded her of the loneliness she often felt, and she had to admit that no matter how much good she could do with her life if she remained single, she would still have to deal with the loneliness.

Forcing herself not to be so concerned for the future, she spent some time catching up on her scripture study and put the matter into the Lord's hands.

PORCUPINE MEATBALLS

1 1/2 lbs. ground beef (not porcupine)
1/2 cup uncooked rice
1 teaspoon salt
1/2 teaspoon pepper
1 tablespoon dry minced onion
1 can tomato soup mixed with 1 can water

Mix first five ingredients and mold into meatballs.
Drop into soup.
Cover and simmer for about an hour, or until rice is
tender.

Chapter 6

Not long after her parents left, Helen answered the phone to hear Shayne's voice. She attempted to quell the fluttering inside her and focus on the reality. He was still married, she reminded herself.

"How are you?" he asked in a way that seemed unusual for their established relationship. He was treating her more like a friend than a baby-sitter. She could live with that, she thought.

"I'm fine. How are you?"

"Not too bad, actually—thanks to you."

"Why me?" she asked, hating the way his praise sent her heart racing.

"You just said all the right things when I needed to hear them."

"Well, I don't know if I can take all the credit for that. I was praying for help, you know."

He laughed softly. "Well then, I'm grateful that you're the kind of woman who helps answer people's prayers. That makes you an angel, doesn't it?" Before she could respond, he laughed again and added, "Oh, but you're a star, aren't you?"

Helen couldn't tell if he was complimenting or

teasing her, so she said nothing. She was relieved when his voice sobered and he went on. "Anyway, I was wondering if you had plans for New Year's Eve."

"Did you need someone to watch the children?" she asked eagerly, thinking of how they could play games and put puzzles together and toast the new year with homemade root beer—if they managed to stay awake that long.

"No," he drawled cautiously, "I was hoping you'd celebrate with us—me and the children, I mean." She was putting together the words to tell him that she didn't think it would be appropriate when he added, "I was thinking we could tell them about the divorce while we're all together, and then if we're having some fun, it will distract them and . . . well, you know."

The silence made Helen realize he was waiting for a response. "Uh . . . well, I'd love to, but . . ."

"But?" he pressed, reminding her of Carla.

"Well," she cleared her throat, "it's like you told me once, we don't want to do anything that might even appear inappropriate."

"But I was married then," he said so matter-of-factly that it took Helen off guard.

Needing clarification, she asked, "What are you saying?" If he thought that having divorce papers in his hand constituted being divorced, he was quite wrong. And she was ready to tell him so.

"I'm saying that I'm divorced. It's over. She had everything in order. It wasn't contested, and we've been separated for months. It's signed and final."

"Really?" she heard herself say, wishing it hadn't sounded so cheerful. Suddenly the entire perspective changed. He was single. He was adorable. And he was asking her to spend New Year's Eve with him—and his children, of course.

"Really," he said. Then he laughed.

"And you sound happy."

"Actually," he admitted, "the things you said to me really made sense. I've spent so many years trying to hold together a dysfunctional marriage that I can't help feeling relieved now that it's over. I know that probably sounds calloused, in a way, but I suppose a part of me has been mourning the failure of the marriage ever since she left. Deep down, I think I knew it would come to this, no matter how badly I wanted it to be otherwise. So now that it's over, it's like . . . I have nothing more to fear. I certainly have some tender spots over it, and I confess I've cried a lot of tears these last few days. But it is time to go forward, and I know I have the Lord's blessings with me. So, I want to celebrate. A new year. A new life. And I want to celebrate with you—because you have made such a difference to all of us." He sighed loudly. "So, what do you say? Will you help me tell the children, and then we'll . . . I don't know . . . we'll do whatever you want."

"How about if you come over here," Helen said quickly. "I'll cook dinner and find some things to do that the kids will enjoy. They can spend the night if they don't make it until midnight, and you can pick them up the next morning."

"That sounds great. Can I bring anything?"

"Dessert," she said decisively. "You're in charge of dessert. Oh, and pick up a chunk of dry ice. We're going to make homemade root beer. It's a tradition in my family."

"That sounds great," he said. "We'll be there . . . when?"

"How about six-thirty?"

"On the dot," he said, and Helen managed to hang up the phone before she let out a delighted little whoop toward the ceiling.

Through the remainder of the day, she kept reminding herself that she had no indication that Shayne felt anything for her beyond friendship. That was fine; he was a good man, and she could thoroughly appreciate having such a friend. And even if more were to come of their relationship, it needed time. But for now, she would enjoy every minute she could with Tamara and Scotty and their adorable father.

The time went quickly as Helen prepared for her little New Year's Eve party. She actually hung crepe paper and got some balloons, as well as little hats and noisemakers. She considered confetti, but knew she'd be vacuuming it up until the Fourth of July. So she settled on paper serpentines instead. She prepared all of the food for a baked potato and salad bar, and made certain the spare bedrooms were ready for Scotty and Tamara.

Then, when she saw that she still had a little extra time, Helen decided to get busy and just mix up the fruitcake she'd been intending to get to since the week before Christmas. She was surprised at how quickly it went together, and wondered why she'd been putting it off. She had it in the oven and the mess cleaned up before the doorbell rang.

The children squealed with excitement when they entered her home and saw the decorations. Helen silently leapt for joy to see Shayne Brynner smile at her as he handed over a bag that contained the makings of banana splits. Together they mixed up the root beer and added the dry ice. The children laughed to see it smoke and bubble.

"Now, by the time we get supper on, we can drink some. And by the time we're ready to toast New Year's, it will be slushy and bubbly."

Helen gave them instructions on helping her set out all they needed for supper on the bar, while she got the potatoes out of the oven without disturbing the fruitcake.

"Something smells good," Shayne said.

"It's fruitcake," she informed him.

"Fruitcake?" he replied, comically feigning disgust. "Like I said, fruitcake has a pretty bad reputation, you know. I can only hope that with *your* reputation in the kitchen, we'll be pleasantly surprised."

"Oh, you will be," she said. "It's my mother's recipe. It's moist and luscious. Not dry and sickly sweet. I promise."

"Ooh, I can't wait," he said, then glanced over the meal laid out. "It looks wonderful. As always, your cooking is superb."

"You're too kind," she said, feeling a giddy flutter inside from the warm glance he gave her. She reminded herself to keep a level head as they all took their plates to the table and Helen asked Shayne if he would choose someone to say the blessing. He chose her.

Helen took a deep breath and offered a sincere blessing over the food, expressing gratitude for all they had been blessed with. The meal passed with the usual small talk and trivialities. When the children were finished and asked if they could have banana splits now, Shayne passed Helen a cautious glance as he said, "There's something important we need to talk about first. After we talk, then we'll make banana splits."

"Is it about Mommy?" Scotty asked.

"Yes, Scooter," Shayne said, "it's about Mommy."

"Is she going to die?" Tamara asked. "'Cause Heather at school, her daddy died."

"No, Snickerdoodle," Shayne said, "Mommy is not going to die. But you know that Mommy hasn't lived with us for a long time now." He glanced toward Helen for support. She nodded firmly as if to tell him he was doing just fine. "I'm not sure why Mommy doesn't want to live with us, but I know it's not because of anything the two of you have done. You're very good children."

"Maybe it's because Mommy's sick," Tamara suggested.

"I think that's part of it," Shayne said. "But the thing is, Mommy has let me know that she's not going to live with us . . . ever again."

"Not ever?" Scotty asked, and tears immediately welled into his big eyes.

"No, Scotty," Shayne took his hand across the table, "not ever."

"Doesn't she like us anymore?" Tamara asked while her tears appeared, too.

Shayne took her hand as well. "I think maybe she doesn't like *me* anymore. Or maybe she just feels like the two of us don't agree on some very important things. So we felt it was best for us not to be married anymore."

"Are you going to get a divorce?" Scotty asked, his voice quivering.

"We already did, son. Mommy and I aren't married anymore. And I should have told you sooner, but I only knew for certain just a few days ago. I know it's hard; it's hard for all of us. But you must remember that no matter what, she is your mom and she loves both of you. It's just not possible for her to live with us anymore. Maybe when you get older, she'll be able to explain the reasons and help you understand better. But for now, we'll just keep on going like we have been, and we'll get along just fine. By next summer we'll be able to buy a house again, and Mommy said that you can go and visit her at Grandma's every once in a while and stay a few days."

The children nodded and sniffled. Shayne pushed back his chair and motioned for them to come into his arms. He hugged them tightly while they all cried. Helen sat at the other end of the table, shedding a few tears of her own. She felt as if she was somehow viewing the situation from a distance, like some kind of bystander, until Shayne looked up at her over the children's heads. He gave her a serene smile, and she felt better. No matter what the future held, she believed that he would allow her to always be a part of the children's lives.

The children perked up as they worked together to clear the table and put the food away, then Helen cut the bananas and Shayne scooped the ice cream. While Helen got the fruitcake out of the oven, the children sat on bar stools and drizzled different flavored syrups over their ice cream, then their father squirted whipped cream on it from a can. Helen declared that she'd wait until later for ice cream, since she'd stuffed herself with her supper. While she was loading the dishwasher, Shayne came up beside her, saying quietly, "Thank you."

"I didn't do anything," she said. "You handled it just fine."

"You were there, and I knew that if I started to bawl or blow it, you'd save me. You provided the perfect atmosphere."

"Well, I'm sure they'll have their moments of grief . . . as you will. But you'll all be just fine."

"Yes, I believe we will." He paused and added, "Where did you learn to be so wise?"

"Am I?" She looked surprised. "Just common sense, I guess."

"No," he said intently, with eyes to match his voice, making Helen's stomach quiver. "It's more than that." For a moment she allowed herself to become lost in his eyes, wondering what it might be like if he ever came to feel about her the way she felt about him. Then she forced herself back to the moment and continued with her chore.

Shayne declared he couldn't wait another minute to taste this fruitcake she'd been bragging about. And he agreed that it was the best he'd ever tasted. The children were too full of ice cream to care. But Helen thoroughly enjoyed the warm, spicy cake since it reminded her so much of holidays when she was a child. Just the smell took her back in time.

Through the evening they played simple board games and card games, laughing and teasing as if nothing in the world was wrong. Helen found herself imagining what it might be like if life could always be this way—if they could actually be a family. Then she scolded herself—once again—for letting her imagination run away with her. She reminded herself that she was very blessed and had much to be thankful for, and she would be content and happy with whatever the Lord blessed her with in the future. And if that was a life as a single woman, she would make it a marvelous one—just as Aunt Libby had.

Later in the evening, Helen pulled out some chips and popcorn—and more root beer. In the middle of a rousing game of Uno, Tamara asked without preamble, "Can Helen be our mother now?"

Helen managed to avoid spitting root beer across the table by clapping a hand over her mouth. She noticed Shayne smirking, and left it up to him to give a reasonable explanation since she was coping with the root beer that had gone up her nose. She nearly had it under control when Shayne said matter-of-factly, "Only if she wants to, of course."

Helen managed to toss him a wary glance while she was choking. But the teasing she had expected to see in his eyes was completely absent. *He was serious!*

When Helen couldn't get control of her coughing, she hurried to the bathroom, grateful for an excuse to leave the table and get hold of her senses. With the door locked between herself and the man who had just implied a marriage proposal, she took a deep breath and gradually managed to stop coughing. Then she pressed her face against the counter as the blood suddenly rushed from her head. Surely he wasn't serious! But that look in his eyes when he'd said it! What was she to make of that? All of her silly fantasies about having him share these feelings suddenly swirled into a hurricane of fear. This was too fast; too *ridiculous!*

Helen reminded herself to remain calm and not blow this out of proportion. She was accustomed to facing problems head-on. She couldn't stay in the bathroom much longer without making the situation all the more awkward. Taking a deep breath, she settled a strategy in her mind and went out to face him, at the same time attempting to quell the swarm of butterflies in her stomach. She found Shayne and the children waiting for her to take her turn at Uno, and forced herself to sit down and do just that. She knew it was important to talk with Shayne and clarify where she stood, but now was not the time. In her opinion, too much had already been said in front of the children.

When the game ended, Shayne suggested that the children go and get ready for bed, then they could count down to midnight while they worked on a simple jigsaw puzzle that Helen had left on the coffee table. The children scurried down the hall while Helen wondered if he sensed the need to clear the air and had purposely initiated a private moment. Helen glanced at him and felt unnerved by his expression. She quickly gathered some snack dishes from the table and hurried to the kitchen, wondering where her resolve to face it head-on had disappeared to.

"Helen," she heard him say in a tender voice that made her already-quivering stomach threaten to burst.

"Yes," she said and proceeded to load their snack dishes into the dishwasher, hoping to avoid eye contact. She was contemplating a way to scold him for saying something in front of the children to imply that she would become a permanent part of their lives. He had no right to make such assumptions. In spite of how she felt about him, *he* didn't know that.

"Forgive me. I shouldn't have said something like that—especially in front of the children."

Feeling immense relief at not having to voice that thought herself, Helen simply said, "I'll have to agree with that." When he said nothing more, she filled in the silence by adding, "You have no idea where my feelings are, or what's going on in my life. To imply to the children that I will be something more in their life than I already am is just . . . well, it's not fair."

"You're right," he said, his tone subtly sheepish. "About the children, that is."

Helen looked up abruptly, wondering what he was implying. She was about to demand an explanation when he continued.

"It's true that I don't know a great deal about you—in a technical sense, at least. But I know that you had nowhere to be for Christmas, and no one special to be with beyond your parents, who live in another state. I know that your life was empty enough that caring for my children has given you a great deal of enjoyment and—dare I guess?—fulfillment. And as far as your feelings go . . . well, forgive me for being presumptuous, Helen, but what am I supposed to make of that look on your face whenever we make eye contact?"

Helen was so aghast she could only gape at him. She reminded herself to close her mouth while she considered how to respond. She had to give him credit for being perceptive, and she wasn't about to deny her feelings and make an even bigger fool of herself. But still, she had to counter with, "Whatever you may or may not believe about me, Mr. Brynner, you *are* being presumptuous."

"Yes," he admitted, "and I'm sorry for that. But . . ."

The children came noisily into the kitchen, halting the conversation abruptly. Helen sensed her own frustration in Shayne's eyes, and she was grateful when he quickly remedied the problem by saying, "Boy, that was fast! Why don't the two of you go start working on that puzzle. You can find all of the edge pieces and start putting them together. Helen and I need to talk privately for a few minutes."

Once the children had calculated that it was still over an hour until midnight, they went to the family room, leaving Helen alone with this man and her feelings for him that suddenly seemed more powerful than anything she'd ever felt in her life.

Trying to get a grip and take up where they'd left off, Helen urged, "But?"

Shayne chuckled and glanced briefly toward the floor as he stuffed his hands into the pockets of his jeans. "But . . ." he repeated, "I would like to explain myself."

When he hesitated, she said, "I'm listening." Her calm tone of voice didn't betray the way her heart was pounding, as if it sensed where this was headed.

"I realize that the ink on my divorce papers is barely dry. But the fact is, I've been separated from my wife for a very long time—several months, physically, and . . . well, as I've recently realized, we've been separated emotionally for years. Once I came to terms with what was happening, I found that the adjustment wasn't too difficult. The only adjustment for me is . . . well, the realization that now I can stop trying to force thoughts of you out of my head."

Helen sucked in her breath. What was he saying? Abruptly she turned her back to him, as if it could help her see this more clearly. Her thoughts roiled helplessly while the silence grew long and awkward. She was actually startled when he cleared his throat gently and said, "Helen, I know I'm probably sounding like a fool, and I know this all seems very fast, but . . . I have to say what I feel, and . . . somehow I know that I'm not feeling this way alone." When Helen still said nothing, he chuckled uncomfortably. "Could you say something . . . *anything?* If you want me to just hit the road, say so. If I'm assuming something that's simply ridiculous, then by all means—"

"It's not ridiculous," she said, but kept her back turned. "It's just that . . . well, as I see it, you're on the rebound here." Helen took a deep breath and forced herself to voice her concerns. She would not allow herself to be set up for a huge disappointment when he eventually realized that his feelings were not based in reality. "I'm around," she said. "I'm convenient. It's not difficult to imagine playing house together when I care for your children and you come home every evening to find me there with supper on the table. But that doesn't necessarily mean that anything more is right for either one of us. What you're feeling is likely nothing more than—"

"No," he said and took hold of her shoulders, forcing her to face him, "you don't know what I'm feeling."

"Why don't you tell me?" she said in a whisper, suddenly hoping with every fiber of her being that he would prove her theory wrong. Looking into his eyes, she wanted him to fall helplessly and hopelessly in love with her. She wanted to spend the rest of her life sharing the ins and outs of everyday life with this man. And it was the intensity of her feelings that frightened her most of all. What had happened to that contentment with the prospect of being single the rest of her life? It was evident that her heart was already lost. But what would she do if he broke it?

"All right, I will," he said firmly. "I'm in love with you, Helen Starkey." She gasped and he added, "And don't tell me about my being on the rebound and how convenient this is. That doesn't change how I feel."

Helen attempted to absorb what he was saying. The intensity in his eyes made her almost believe him. But there was a glimmer of fear that made her hesitate. She knew she had a lot to offer, and she had the ability to make him happy. But there were so many matters about which she had no idea how he felt. Her weight, for one thing. She was happy with herself, knowing that she was healthy and did her best to stay that way. But she wouldn't spend the rest of her life with a man who thought she would be more valuable if she was thin. Reminding herself that there was plenty of time to explore their views on such matters, she forced her voice enough to say, "Feelings alone don't make a good relationship, Mr. Brynner."

"My name is Shayne," he said with an edge of frustration to his voice. "You're not just a nanny-slash-housekeeper to me, as you so quaintly put it. At the very least, we are friends, and no matter what comes of this, we always will be. Now, in order to make myself perfectly clear, perhaps I should tell you where I'm coming from."

"Perhaps you should," she said, wishing it hadn't sounded so formal.

"When the reality finally sank in that my marriage was over, the despair I felt was indescribable. I prayed half the night to find peace and hope and the ability to get through this. The peace came as I recalled the words you'd said to me that made so much sense, and I felt the Spirit confirm their truth. It was time for me to get beyond this and build a new life. The hope came in the same moment when it became evident that God had sent a star to me long before I knew I needed one; a star to guide me through the darkness to that new life. I couldn't imagine what I'd ever done to warrant the blessing of having someone like you already in my life."

"But you hardly know me," she said in little more than a whisper.

"Oh, but I do. You're beautiful. You're wise. You're organized and efficient. You're caring and compassionate. You're successful in a career that has more meaning than most in this world. You have a testimony of the gospel that humbles me. You're a marvelous cook, and . . . did I mention that you're beautiful? And I told myself that I'd be the world's biggest fool if I didn't recognize the opportunity before me. But all that would mean nothing, Helen, if it weren't for the feelings that have come to life inside of me. I know the situation warrants time and careful consideration. But I would be an even bigger fool if I let another day go by without letting you know how I feel, Helen, and I can only hope and pray that something inside of you cares for me, too.

Either way, I want you to always be a part of the children's lives. They love you and they need you. The thing is . . . I love you and need you, too."

Helen didn't realize she was crying until he reached up and wiped her tears away with his fingers. He'd managed to counter her every argument—even the ones she hadn't voiced. And the reality of his feelings left her elated; humbled, in awe, ecstatic, and just plain elated. Not to mention deliriously happy.

Unable to bear the gaze in his eyes, and not knowing what to say, she pressed her head to his shoulder and moved effortlessly into his embrace. She felt him sigh, as if the gesture had somehow relieved his anxiety. But it was evident his confessions had left him vulnerable when he said, "You must have something to say. You don't have to spare my feelings, but for the love of heaven, don't leave me wondering where I stand."

Helen came up with a dozen reasons to hold her feelings back, but they all had to do with fear. He had poured his heart out to her in good faith, and she owed him the same degree of honesty. Instinctively she tightened her hold on him and murmured, "I love you, too . . . Shayne."

She felt him laugh as he hugged her tighter, practically lifting her off the floor. Helen couldn't remember the last time she'd been embraced by a man—except her father or brothers. And it felt so incredibly wonderful. She forced away her fears that this might not last and made up her mind to take it one day at a time. She became so lost in the moment that she almost felt as if she was dreaming. But the reality became clear when she felt his lips against her forehead. Feeling as if she could stay in his arms forever, she was startled by the children's laughter coming from the other room. Abruptly she stepped back and chuckled tensely. "We hadn't better let the children catch us like this," she said, unable to keep from looking at him as his eyes seemed to echo every-thing he'd just said to her. "At least not yet; not until . . . we're sure. You know what I mean."

Shayne nodded and smiled, and Helen wanted to believe that it would only be a matter of time before she became a part of their family. The very idea seemed like a dream come true, and she prayed in her heart that this was not just a cloak for some unforeseen trial, meant to make her stronger.

Helen hurried into the front room, fearing she couldn't bear the enormity of her feelings another second with him watching her that way. Shayne followed her, and they worked together to help the chil-dren put the puzzle together. When they were finished, it became evident that Tamara was getting sleepy. They turned on the television and watched the countdown, while Tamara drifted off to sleep with her head in her father's lap. Scotty soon followed her into slumber, leaning against Helen's arm.

"Happy New Year," Shayne said with a chuckle when midnight hit and the children were oblivious.

"Happy New Year," she repeated, and was surprised when he reached over and kissed her quickly. It was so brief that she might have thought she'd imagined it, except for the electrifying response she felt from his lips touching hers. He smiled with something deep and warm showing in his eyes, then he carried the children to the beds they would sleep in.

"Well, I guess I should be on my way," Shayne said, walking toward the front door after they were all tucked in. He turned toward her with his hand on the knob. "Will I see you tomorrow . . . beyond getting the children back, I mean?"

"I was going to cook a turkey. It's tradition, you know. For me, it just doesn't seem like New Year's Day without a turkey. You can't expect me to eat it all alone."

Shayne smiled. "It sounds wonderful. Can I bring anything?"

"Just your charming and adorable self," she said, delighted with the opportunity to put a voice to what she'd been feeling. He looked pleasantly surprised by the comment before he kissed her forehead and left for the night. For fear of waking the children, Helen resisted the urge to let out a whoop of pure joy. Instead, she crawled into her bed, feeling happier than she believed she ever had. She only prayed it would last.

MOTHER'S FRUITCAKE

1 3/4 cups flour
1/4 teaspoon salt
1/2 teaspoon cinnamon
1/2 teaspoon cloves
1/2 cup shortening
1 teaspoon vanilla
1 cup sugar
1 egg
1/2 cup each of raisins and chopped nuts
1/2 teaspoon soda dissolved in 1 cup
hot applesauce
1 pound candied fruit

Cream together shortening, sugar, egg, and vanilla. Add applesauce mixture.

Mix together dry ingredients and add, along with nuts and raisins. Then add fruit. Bake in loaf pan at 325° for one hour.

Chapter 7

In Helen's opinion, New Year's Day was—so far—the happiest day of her life. It was easy to imagine every holiday being this way. The children seemed content and comfortable, and occasionally Shayne would send her a glance that filled her with a deep thrill. His feelings for her were evident, and she wondered why she should be so blessed.

The following Sunday she declined Shayne's offer to take her to church with them, since she had to teach her Primary class. But she went to the apartment after meetings were over and quickly declared that she needed to go grocery shopping on his behalf the very next day. They enjoyed soup and grilled cheese sandwiches, then Helen surveyed the cupboards to assess the available ingredients before she announced, "I think we should make a coffee cake."

"Coffee cake?" Scotty questioned with a wrinkle of his nose. Helen smiled to note how thoroughly he looked like his father.

"I hope it doesn't have coffee in it," Tamara said. "Because we're not supposed to drink coffee."

"No," Helen assured her, "there's no coffee in it. They call it coffee cake because a lot of people like to eat it with their coffee. But we can eat it with cocoa instead. How does that sound?"

"I like cake," Tamara declared.

Helen let the children help her mix up the simple recipe. In fact, they made a double batch so there would be some left tomorrow.

"If Dad doesn't eat it for breakfast," Scotty said as they were putting it in the oven. "Dad always eats the good stuff for breakfast."

Shayne winked at Helen as he filled the teapot to put some water on to boil for cocoa. "I'd much rather eat Helen's leftovers for breakfast than that dry, crunchy stuff you guys like."

After they'd shared coffee cake and cocoa, Helen was surprised to hear Shayne say, "Would you like to stay for scripture study?"

"I'd love to," she said. Sitting with the family as they took turns reading from the Book of Mormon, she felt her contentment deepen. She prayed with all her heart that this was the beginning of the rest of her life, and not just a dream.

Helen stayed until the children were tucked into bed, then she was quick to say, "I should be going."

"Do you have something you need to do?" Shayne asked with obvious disappointment.

"Not really, but . . ." She chuckled at herself and had to clarify. "I guess I've got to get out of the habit of thinking that you're married and . . . well, you know."

"Yes, I know," he said, taking her hand and leading her to the couch. Helen felt electricity from his touch, an excitement that deepened when he sat close beside her and kept her hand in his. He'd been especially careful not to show his affection around the children, but now that they were asleep, she felt certain he was making it clear that the feelings he'd confessed had not changed.

"Now," he said, "it's time I got to know you better. I want your life story. Start at the very beginning."

Helen laughed. "You'll be bored senseless."

"Nonsense." He laughed with her. "I want to hear everything."

Helen started with the bare facts of her childhood, but he continually asked questions that prompted her to share details and stories of growing up in a small town in Idaho, where her father owned a hardware store and her mother had taught school. With his urging she continued through her teen years, then talked of her mission and her college education. She was amazed at how completely relaxed she felt with him, and his genuine interest in her prompted the sharing of memories that warmed her.

"So, what brought you to Utah?" he asked. "If your brothers are all settled near your parents, why did you come here?"

"Well," she drawled, "it was just something I felt I needed to do. You see, I love my family, and they mean well. But everyone seemed to be terribly preoccupied with the fact that I wasn't married and how they could help rectify it. I needed to establish myself without that kind of pressure always hanging over me."

"You've established yourself well, obviously," he said with admiration in his eyes. "And now?"

"What do you mean by that?"

"Well . . . I guess I'm asking: are you content being single?"

Helen took a deep breath, wanting to express herself appropriately, considering their growing affection and the possibilities of the future that he'd implied. "I'm happy," she said firmly. "I admit that I've often felt something was missing, but I've never been unhappy because of it. I enjoy my work, and . . . well, caring for Scotty and Tamara has brought a great deal of fulfillment into my life. And I must admit that your Aunt Libby left a deep impression on me. Her example made me realize that I could stay single and live a full life."

"She's an incredible woman," Shayne said, "but no more incredible than you."

Helen warmed to the compliment but glanced away, feeling suddenly self-conscious at all the attention he'd been giving her.

"Why didn't you ever get married?" he asked, his boldness taking her off guard. When she hesitated to answer, he added, "I mean . . . I don't understand how someone as talented and beautiful as you could make it this far without being snatched up."

She relaxed a little. "The right opportunity never presented itself. I dated quite a bit, even had a few proposals. But I just knew it wasn't right."

"Well, I'm glad you didn't get snatched up," he said. "But," he added, seeming slightly tense, "I guess what I want to know is: are you content to stay single . . . now?"

"Now?"

"Now that you're in love with me," he said.

He laughed softly, but as Helen looked into his eyes, his expression became as serious as she felt. She chose her words very carefully. "I'm willing to live my life in the way that's best for me. I'm certain that with time, I'll know what's best."

His penetrating gaze seemed to reflect her own hope that they would indeed be together. She became completely mesmerized by his gaze, as if she could almost literally see eternity in his eyes. She didn't feel the least bit surprised when he bent to kiss her. It seemed the most natural thing in the world to be with him this way. As their lips met, she felt the contentment of her life deepen.

"I love you, Helen," he murmured, touching her hair with gentle fingers. He kissed her again, then drew back to look into her eyes. With a subtle quiver in his voice, he said, "Do you have any idea how you have blessed my life? When things fell apart with Margie, I kept hanging on to the hope that somehow we could work it out and be happy. I loved her, Helen. I loved her so much." The tremor in his voice deepened. "I think I knew for a long time that divorce was inevitable, but I didn't want to face it. When it finally happened, I felt as if part of my heart had been cut out. Then I realized that it had been cut out years ago. I just hadn't been willing to admit it. And you were right there, right beside me, when I needed you most. You made me believe in myself again without even trying. You helped me know in my heart that I'd done all I could do. Without even saying anything, your kindness and caring made me believe in love again." He kissed her once more. "Thank you, Helen."

Helen smiled and touched his face, marveling at the feel of his stubbled skin. "Thank *you,*" she said.

"For what?" he asked, touching his nose to hers.

"For . . . letting me be there. For letting me love your kids. And . . . for falling in love with me." She didn't add that she felt certain whether they married or not, his affection for her still meant more than she could ever describe.

Shayne laughed softly as he drew away. She could almost feel him consciously keeping himself within appropriate boundaries, and she admired him for it. When silence persisted, she began asking him questions about his own childhood. They talked for another hour, while Helen felt her admiration and respect growing deeper. She loved hearing about his family, his mission, his work, and his obvious love of the gospel and the way he used it in his life.

Time slipped easily by until Helen felt herself yawning and thought to glance at her watch. "Good heavens," she said, "we've both got work in the morning, and it's well past eleven."

Shayne walked her to her car and left her with a kiss, insisting that she call him when she got home. She did, and they talked another hour before she sank into an exhausted, delighted slumber.

<hr />

Returning to school after the holidays was full of the usual challenges. It was always difficult to settle the children back into their routine after the long break. And the weather on that first day back was especially cold and snowy, although Helen felt warm inside. Lunchtime was the first opportunity Helen had to talk to Carla.

"So, how were your holidays?" Helen asked just before she bit into a turkey sandwich on whole wheat.

"Great," Carla said, then she laughed. "Exhausting, but great. How about you?"

"The same," Helen said, feeling a delightful tremor inside as she thought of how her life had changed since they'd last shared lunch together.

She knew she wouldn't be able to hold on to her secret for long when Carla stopped chewing to stare at her a moment before she demanded, "What's up?"

"What makes you think something's up?"

"It's that perma-grin you're wearing," Carla insisted. "You've been smiling ever since you got here this morning—at least when I've seen you. So what's up?"

"Well," Helen drawled, wondering where to begin, "for starters, Shayne's divorce is final."

"Already?"

"Yeah. They'd been separated a long time. It didn't take much to make it final."

"Wow," Carla said, turning to give her a sidelong glance. "So . . . does this perma-grin have something to do with him?"

"Yes," Helen replied, turning the word into a giggle.

"He asked you out?"

"Oh, more than that."

"Well, what?" Carla demanded, too impatient to wait for Helen to take another bite and chew it.

"Well, it all started on New Year's Eve when . . ." Helen giggled again, recalling how she'd responded initially to Shayne's unexpected statement. Looking back, it seemed terribly funny.

"Do I have to strangle you to get you to talk?" Carla hissed in a quiet voice.

"All right. All right," Helen said. "After he told the

kids about the divorce, Tamara asked if I could be their mother now, and . . ." Helen chuckled again. "Shayne said . . ." She lowered her voice to mimic him. "'. . . Only if she wants to, of course.'"

"You're joking."

"No. I'm quite serious."

"What did you do?"

"After I recovered from the root beer spraying out my nose, you mean?"

Carla laughed loudly. "Yeah, after that."

"Well, at first I was completely thrown off, and a little upset with his approach. But when we talked, I realized he was being sincere, and his heart's in the right place. He loves me." Helen let out a delighted little laugh at just hearing it spoken. "And I love him."

"But . . . it's so soon," Carla said with a grin that made it evident she was more happy than concerned.

"Well, nothing's official. We've agreed to give it some time, but . . . well, I'm happy. What can I say?"

They had to hurry to eat and gather up their little flocks from the snowy playground, but after school, while the children did their homework, Helen quietly told Carla more about her feelings, and how her confusion had quickly melted away.

Through the next few weeks, Tamara and Scotty had no trouble adjusting to having Helen around most of the time. They didn't seem to even notice when Shayne started holding her hand or putting his arm around her in their presence. And Helen became so thoroughly comfortable with Shayne that it seemed there was no other option besides being together—forever.

Helen loved sharing the children with him, and she

enjoyed every minute that they worked and played together. Occasionally the children fought with each other or got whiny, but she was pleased with the way Shayne handled it. The evidence continued to deepen that he was a good man.

Margie made regular calls to talk to the children, and they often told her they missed her. But as they shared and discussed their feelings with Helen and Shayne, they seemed to be able to talk to their mother without getting upset.

As much as Helen enjoyed being all together as a family, she thoroughly loved the time she had with Shayne in the evenings after the children had gone to bed. It seemed they never ran out of things to talk about. Once a week he made a point of getting a sitter for the children so the two of them could go out on a "real date" as he called it. He managed to make her feel like a queen, without being showy or overzealous. They studied the scriptures together every day, and gradually their conversations turned more and more to the prospect of a temple marriage and the life they would share. Although it had never been voiced officially, Helen knew beyond any doubt that it would happen. And her happiness was beyond description.

The last week of January was especially cold, and Helen took the children more often to her house after school. She'd build a fire in the fireplace, and the coziness of its warmth emphasized the feelings growing in her heart. It seemed so perfectly natural to have Shayne come home to greet her with a kiss, and they'd discuss their day over the supper table.

On a particularly cold night, Tamara asked as she was finishing her second helping of porcupine meatballs, "Daddy, are you going to marry Helen?"

Shayne didn't seem at all surprised by the question. He just smiled and said, "Well, Snickerdoodle, I certainly want to. But marriage is a very important decision. It's something we need to pray about, and we need to take some time to be absolutely certain we can always make each other happy."

"Can I pray about it, too?" Tamara asked.

Shayne looked briefly puzzled and glanced at Helen, as if he'd like her to handle that one.

"Of course you can, honey," Helen said. "But it's your father and I who will be getting married if it's right, so we are the ones who need to get the answer. But you can pray that everything will work out for the best."

"Okay," Tamara said, then she immediately left the table as if she was going to go do it right this minute.

"How do you feel about that, Scotty?" Shayne asked him.

"I like Helen," he said.

"I like her too," Shayne said, winking at Helen. "But how do you feel about all of us being a family?"

"I miss Mom sometimes, but . . . I want Helen to live with us. Except we should live with Helen, 'cause her house is bigger."

Helen felt warmed by Shayne's smile. He simply said, "We'll just have to see."

A minute later, Tamara returned and stood right next to her father. "Daddy," she said, "when you propose to Helen, are you going to go down on one knee?"

Shayne chuckled. "I don't know, Tamara. Like I told Scotty, we'll just have to see."

"Okay," she said, then Helen had the children help clear the table.

After they'd gone off to play, Shayne helped Helen with the dishes. They were working in contemplative silence until he said, "So, if I do actually propose to you, Miss Star, how do you think I should do it?"

Helen chuckled. "I thought that was the man's department."

"Maybe, but . . . well, don't you have some great fantasy about being proposed to?"

"Not really," she said. "As long as it's the right man with the right question, I don't suppose it matters much."

"Okay, but humor me. What kind of things do you like? Flowers, chocolates, cupcakes?"

Helen laughed. "Cupcakes, yes. Those kind you buy at the store bakery with the fluffy frosting on top. Although I probably *shouldn't* want cupcakes. They'd just go to my hips. My kids at school, though, they'd love cupcakes."

"But, what would *you* love?"

"You mentioned chocolate. Chocolate is good. Again, I probably shouldn't. But hey, life is short. I deserve chocolates now and then."

"That's the spirit," he said with a tender laugh, then he reached over and kissed her. Helen could never tell him what his attitude meant to her. She'd never had the slightest indication that her weight bothered him. In fact, it was plainly evident simply by the way he looked at her that he loved her just the way she was. "Okay," he went on, "what about flowers . . . hypothetically speaking, of course."

"Oh, I love flowers," she said. "Roses, especially. There's nothing like them, is there? And they are the symbol of love. Flowers are nice."

"What color?"

"What is this? A poll?"

"Maybe. What color?"

"Any color. I just love roses."

"Okay, what else?"

"I don't know," she insisted. "This is silly."

"How about balloons?"

"Balloons are good. They certainly would get my attention. But I like the cupcake idea the best. Just stick that ring in a cupcake."

She laughed, and he pulled her into his arms. "I just might do that, but . . . I'm afraid you'd swallow it by mistake."

"I have an idea. *If* you decide you want to propose, just do it, okay? Like I said—right man. Right question. That's all that matters."

"I can't propose until I know you'll say yes. Otherwise, well . . . you know."

Helen smiled and kissed his nose. She wanted to tell him the "yes" part wasn't a concern. She knew beyond any doubt that marrying him was the right thing. But she didn't want to seem too pushy, so she just said, "I don't think that will be a problem." She touched his face. "I think you know how I feel."

He smiled and kissed her, only to be interrupted by Scotty and Tamara arguing in the other room. Shayne went to referee, and Helen uttered a silent prayer of thanks for being guided into Shayne Brynner's life.

COFFEE CAKE

1 cup pancake mix
1/3 cup sugar
1/3 cup milk
1 egg
1/4 cup butter, melted

Mix together and pour into greased eight-inch round pan. Mix ingredients for topping until crumbly. Sprinkle over top of batter and bake at 375° for 20 minutes.

Topping:
1/4 cup brown sugar
1/4 cup flour
1/4 teaspoon cinnamon
2 tablespoons melted butter

Don't add any coffee! Eat with cocoa!!

Chapter 8

Helen couldn't remember the last time she'd actually looked forward to Valentine's Day. Shayne had made arrangements for the children so he could take her out for a nice dinner, and she couldn't help hoping that an official proposal might be on the agenda.

The school day seemed to drag, but while the children were cutting out construction paper hearts and paper doilies to make valentines for their parents, Helen thought of what awaited her this evening and felt a delightful tremor move through her. One side of the room was lined with decorated shoe boxes, all ready for the exchange of valentines among the children. The room mothers would be arriving in less than an hour, bringing the makings of a class party, according to tradition. She was startled when a voice came over the intercom saying, "Miss Star, could you send Scotty Brynner to the office for just a minute, please."

"Yes, of course," Helen called back, then she nodded toward Scotty, who looked startled, and perhaps a little nervous. "I'm sure it's nothing," she whispered as he walked past her. "You can finish your valentine for your dad when you get back."

Scotty nodded and hurried into the hall. Feeling a more personal responsibility for Scotty, Helen wondered what might be happening. Her heart quickened at the thought that perhaps it was some kind of emergency involving his father. Five minutes later, she was nearly ready to go to the office herself and see what was going on. Then she looked up to see Scotty coming into the room carrying a large, flat bakery box.

"Hi," he said with a grin that nearly broke his face. "My dad sent this." He set it on her desk with a heavy sigh, as if balancing the large box had taken a great deal of energy. "He said the one in the middle is for you."

"Oh, really?" Helen chuckled and peeked inside the box while all of the children moved gingerly closer, buzzing with curiosity. She laughed as she pulled off the lid to reveal about three dozen cupcakes with fluffy pink frosting and little heart sprinkles all over them. The children gasped with pleasure, obviously surmising that there were enough to go around. The cupcake in the middle was crowned with a large gold plastic ring, bearing a bright pink heart in the center.

"Oh, look what I get!" Helen said with exaggerated pleasure, tingling to think of Shayne putting it there. She picked up the ring and licked the frosting off it before she put it on her ring finger and showed it off with a dramatic gesture that made the children giggle. Helen felt warmed by the children's excitement. She marveled at Shayne's insight in knowing that a surprise for her would be more fun if it was something she could share with the children. Without a word, his gesture had acknowledged his respect for her work and his desire to please these children who meant so much to her.

"All right," she said, "everyone back to your seats. Get your valentines finished. When the room is clean, we'll all have a cupcake at the beginning of our class party."

The children were barely seated when Tamara entered the room, carrying a large bouquet of helium balloons. "Oh, my goodness!" Helen gasped as she surveyed the collection of brightly colored orbs. There were at least a dozen, in different shades of red and pink, except for one huge white balloon that hovered above the rest—shaped like a star.

Tamara's grin was at least as big as Scotty's had been as she announced, "These are from my dad!"

"Really?" Helen chuckled, then added with light sarcasm, "I never would have guessed." She took the handful of ribbons from Tamara and said, "And where exactly is your father? Did he—"

"I'm right here," Shayne said from the doorway. She looked up to see him holding a bouquet of red and white roses in one arm and a large, heart-shaped box of chocolates in the other. Helen was vaguely aware of the children becoming silent, as if they sensed some kind of momentous occasion. "Happy Valentine's Day," he said, coming toward her. He handed her the flowers and kissed her on the cheek, whispering, "I didn't want to take any chances, so I got some of everything."

Helen chuckled, then her heart quickened as she recalled that their conversation about balloons and cupcakes had been centered on marriage proposals. Since her hands were full of flowers and balloons, he set the box of chocolates on her desk with the cupcakes, then he smiled and winked, making her heart go all the faster. Did he have any idea how adorable he was? How much she loved him?

In spite of her hopes and the evidence of his gifts, Helen could hardly breathe when he went down on one knee and pulled a little black box out of his jacket pocket. "Miss Star," he said loudly enough for everyone to hear, "I've come to ask you if you'll be my wife."

Before Helen could even catch her breath, she heard Scotty and Tamara whispering loudly, "Please say yes! Please say yes!"

Shayne chuckled and glanced briefly toward his children, before turning back to Helen with a gaze so intense it made her knees feel weak. "Of course, yes," she said.

The entire class cheered and applauded, and Shayne laughed as he opened the little box and slid a diamond ring onto her finger—next to the plastic one. He stood and took hold of her shoulders as he kissed her with zeal, which prompted several boys in the room to make dramatic noises of disgust. Helen did her best to hug him, inundated as she was with roses and balloons. But it was impossible to wipe away the tears that trickled from her eyes. Shayne did it for her, then he kissed her again and whispered, "I love you, Helen. You've made me the happiest man alive."

"My happiness is at least as great," she whispered back. Then she laughed and managed to set the roses down carefully after she'd inhaled their sweet fragrance. "I never dreamed I could be so happy."

She was struggling to tie the balloons to the back of her chair when she overheard a child asking Scotty, "Is that your dad?"

"Yep," he replied proudly.

"Then Miss Star is going to be your new mom," another child said, as if they were the only ones who might have figured it out.

"It will be *Mrs.* Star," a girl informed them, who spoke with a lisp. It was evident Shayne had heard as well when she saw him suppressing a chuckle.

"I like that," he said for Helen's ears only. "Mrs. Star."

"Mrs. Brynner, actually."

"I like that even better, but . . . I think it should be Mrs. Star at school." He glanced around the room at its quaint decor. "It's just . . . the way it should be."

Helen just laughed and hugged him tightly, now that her arms were free. Tamara gave Helen a hug and told her dad that she needed to go back to class or she'd miss her party.

"Will you stay for our party?" Helen asked him as Tamara skipped out of the room.

"I'd love to," he said.

Helen managed to get the children to calm down and return to their seats, reminding them that the room mothers would soon be there and they needed to finish their projects. When they were busily working, Helen motioned for Shayne to follow her, and she tiptoed across the hall to peek into Carla's room.

"Hey," she called in a whisper, and Carla came toward the door.

"What's all the racket over there?" Carla asked. "It sounds like you're having more fun than we are, and I don't know if I can live with that. Oh, hi," she said, realizing Shayne was there. "So it was you instigating all that racket! Shame on you!"

"Guilty," he said with a chuckle.

"So, what's up?" Carla asked Helen. "You look happy."

Helen just held up her left hand and Carla gave an exaggerated, "Ooh. I see." Then she added, speaking more to Shayne, "May I say that I'm not terribly surprised?"

"Of course."

"But I'm terribly happy for you," Carla said with a rich laugh as she embraced Helen. "However," she added, taking Helen's hand, "I think I like this ring best." She examined the plastic one as if she were a great authority on fine jewelry.

"Yes, me too," Helen said. "I'll treasure it forever." Moving back toward her classroom, where she could hear the children's voices getting louder, she added, "Come over in a few minutes for a cupcake."

"I'll do that," Carla said. "And . . . congratulations. It's wonderful—for both of you."

"But especially for me," Shayne said with a gaze toward Helen that echoed his words.

The remainder of the day sped by in a whirlwind of perfect bliss. Helen was pleasantly surprised with the way Shayne integrated himself into the classroom as the children finished their valentines and enjoyed their party. The evening was even more wonderful as they shared a fine meal and discussed their plans for the future.

Somewhere in the middle of the main course, Shayne reached across the table to take her hand, fingering the diamond ring she wore. She'd chosen to leave the plastic one at home.

"Helen," he said, "I don't know how much time you need to get ready for a wedding, but I have an opinion I'd like to express about a date."

"Okay," she said, and took a long sip of water.

"I was thinking that it was before Halloween that you came into our lives, and . . . well, it's been a long, difficult winter for me. But you've been like . . . well, forgive the pun, like a star that has guided me through the cold and the darkness. I know it doesn't give us a lot of time, but. . . for a symbolic kind of reason, I was thinking it would be nice to get married on the first day of spring."

Helen smiled. "I think I like that idea, but . . . well, as you said, it's not very far away."

"I'll do everything I can to help," he said. "I want everything to be just the way you want it to be. It's your first—and only—wedding." He smiled widely. "I want it to be perfect. So, if that's not enough time, you just say so."

"I think the first day of spring is great," she said, making no attempt to hide her excitement. "Let me talk to my mother. I'll need to enlist her help. Then we'll call the temple and see what we can do."

Shayne smiled again and kissed her hand before they proceeded to eat. They talked of their plans for him and the children to move into her home. Shayne talked about finishing the basement as if it would be a pleasure, and he offered the money he'd been saving for a down payment to use for wedding expenses and a honeymoon. "If there's any left over," he said, "we'll put it into the house. And with both our incomes, we'll be able to pay off the house much sooner."

They talked about the children they'd have together, and the fun things they would do with Scotty and Tamara. They decided that taking them on a vacation for spring break would be a good idea, since they would be left at home for the honeymoon. Helen felt certain her parents would come and stay with the children while they were gone, and she couldn't wait to get home and call her mother with the news—except that she didn't want to be away from Shayne for even a moment.

Sadie's reaction to the news was beyond Helen's greatest expectations. She was thrilled with the "first day of spring" idea, and felt confident they could get it all done. Helen went to sleep that night amazed with the reality that dreams really did come true.

The phone was ringing when Shayne walked into the apartment after picking up the kids from a neighbor's home. His suspicion that it would be Margie was verified when Tamara answered and said, "Oh, hi Mom." She then rattled off a long list of all the things she had done to celebrate Valentine's Day, ending with the declaration, "And guess what! Daddy's going to marry Miss Star. He proposed to her on one knee in front of the whole class. He brought balloons and cupcakes and flowers and—"

"Tamara," Shayne called softly, "Mommy doesn't need to know all of that."

Tamara looked confused but returned to her conversation, obviously answering questions by her brief comments. Shayne realized his palms were sweating as he wondered how Margie would take all of this. Her calls to the children had been regular and even warm. She'd sent them an occasional package in the mail, including one that had arrived yesterday with some treats, two small stuffed animals, and valentine cards. Thus far, Shayne had been pleased with the results of her relationship with the children. It seemed that long-distance motherhood suited her, and she was doing well at making the children feel that she loved them—better, in some ways, than when she had been living under the same roof. But now there was a new development, and he had no idea how Margie would react. He knew in his heart that nothing could mar the happiness he had found with Helen. Still, he didn't want any complications or hard feelings.

Tamara put Scotty on the phone, and Shayne grimaced as the boy overcame his usually quiet nature to fill in all of the details of his father's relationship with Helen that Tamara had overlooked. He wasn't at all surprised to hear Scotty say, "Hey Dad, Mom wants to talk to you."

Shayne took a deep breath and hurried to say into the phone, "Hi, Margie. Thanks for the stuff you sent. We got it yesterday. The kids loved it."

"No problem," Margie said, actually sounding happy. "So, I hear you're getting married."

"That's right," he said with no tone of apology.

"Isn't this kind of fast?"

He was determined not to justify himself to her or participate in any kind of an argument. He simply said, "I feel I'm doing the right thing."

"Well, that's good then. If I didn't know better, I'd think you'd been fooling around before the divorce was final."

Shayne swallowed hard. "I hope you know better."

"Yes, I do, actually. According to the children, she's perfection personified."

"She's a wonderful woman. Perhaps you'll find someone who . . ." He couldn't resist wording it in a way that responded to her mother's criticism of him. "Someone who can take care of you."

"Perhaps," she said, apparently missing his gibe. "Well, I wish you every happiness," she added in a voice that seemed genuine, but Shayne knew her well enough to catch the subtle vindictive overtone. If he'd had any doubt as to her lack of sincerity, her true character came through as she added, "With any luck, you'll have learned a thing or two, and you'll be able to get it right this time. Otherwise, you're just going to end up losing this wife, too."

Shayne was so stunned he couldn't respond. He could barely breathe. He'd been well aware that Margie was capable of criticizing him deeply; she was not known for her tact or sensitivity. But he'd forgotten how much her words could hurt him. And, though it shouldn't have surprised him, he was freshly amazed at how she could explain away all of the difficulties in their marriage with the simple rationalization that he had been incompetent as a husband.

The silence forced him to his senses. He knew there was no response he could give that wouldn't either provoke an argument, or make him end up looking like a fool. So he simply forced an indifferent tone as he said, "It was nice talking to you, Margie. Happy Valentine's Day."

"You too," she said with an air of disappointment

that told Shayne she would have preferred an argument—or at least some kind of defensive response. At least his indifference had outdone her on that count. But long after he hung up the phone, Shayne felt tainted by the conversation. He could logically review the efforts he had made through the years of his marriage: the fasting, the prayer, the conscious exertion he'd put into examining his character and behavior with the purpose of fine-tuning himself in every way that might make the marriage better. But emotionally, the questions blared at him in neon: *Did you do something that made your marriage fail? Will it happen again? Will you end up hurting Helen in the long run?*

The phone's ringing startled him, then he remembered that he was supposed to call Helen and let her know they'd made it home all right. For a moment he didn't want to answer, as if she might sense his doubts and discover some reason to find him unworthy of her love. Then he realized that she was the only one who could lead him to the light of reason through the fog of his misgivings and fears.

"Hello," he said eagerly, and just her warm response made him feel better. "Sorry I didn't call. Margie called the second we were in the door, and . . ."

"Are you all right?" she asked when he hesitated.

"I think so . . . but I also think I should talk. I know it would be easier to ignore it, but I can't. Does that make sense?"

"Absolutely," she said. Then it was easy for Shayne to say everything he needed to—not just about the phone call and the way it had made him feel, but about all of the attitudes and struggles in his marriage that had made the issue difficult. He actually cried a little as he felt himself taking another step toward putting his failed marriage behind him.

It was late when he finally drifted into sleep. But he slept peacefully, knowing his life was on the right track, and he had a bright future with the smartest, most loving, beautiful woman he had ever known.

The next day, Shayne came home from work to find the children busy with construction paper and glue, and Helen stirring a pot of chili over the stove. For a moment it felt very much like those first weeks she had been helping with the children, when he had barely known her. Still, he felt the same deep gratitude now that he had felt then, and he uttered a silent prayer to express just how grateful he was for the light she had brought into his life.

He greeted her with a kiss, anxious for the day when they would be living together under the same roof. "Mmm," he said, inhaling the steam from the simmering pot. "You must have been cooking ever since you got home."

"Not really; it was easy." She grinned and gave him a tight hug. "I've got more important things to do than spend all afternoon in the kitchen. I've got a wedding to plan."

"How delightful," he said, and kissed her again. The children came running at the sound of his voice, and he laughed as he scooped them into his arms for a proper greeting. He knew life could be no better than this.

BUSY MOM CHILI

Brown 1 lb. ground beef with dried minced onion and garlic to taste.
Drain grease and add the following:

1 28 oz. can tomatoes with liquid
2 teaspoons celery salt
1 tablespoon chili powder
1 teaspoon sugar
1 teaspoon Worcestershire sauce
1 27 oz. can kidney beans, drained
1 8 oz. can tomato sauce

Simmer for one hour. See . . . easy!

Chapter 9

Through the next few weeks, Helen became consumed with wedding plans, involving Shayne and the children as much as possible. Gradually their belongings began filtering into her home, making it truly feel more like home than it ever had. She was grateful now that she'd felt compelled to buy a home larger than she'd needed at the time. Now it would be barely adequate until the basement was finished.

Helen felt so indescribably happy that she often asked herself why she should be so blessed. At moments, it all just seemed too good to be true. She only had to look at Shayne to know that it *was* true, but it soon became evident that nothing good comes without at least one obnoxious fly in the ointment.

Two weeks shy of the wedding, Helen was in her classroom finishing up her preparations for the following day when Ms. Slocum, a fifth-grade teacher, entered the room with what she obviously considered a very important purpose. Helen suppressed a groan of agony and forced a smile. Ms. Slocum was one of the biggest reasons that Helen had been repulsed by the idea of remaining single. Where Aunt Libby's example had been positive, this woman's had been the opposite. She insisted on being called *Ms.* Slocum, since she obviously resented the fact that she was a "Miss" and not a "Mrs." And she had a cynical, bitter aura that showed in the lines of her face, making her appear much older than her fifty-two years. She was often sticking her nose where it didn't belong, and making mountains out of molehills. And now, Helen realized, she had deemed it necessary to make Helen a part of one of her concerns.

"Hello," Helen said as politely as she could manage. "What can I do for you?"

"I wondered if we might have a few minutes." She glanced toward Scotty and Tamara with a subtle glare of disdain. "Alone."

"Of course," Helen said, already not liking this. "Scotty, Tamara," she said, and the children looked up from their homework, "it's a nice day outside. Why don't you go out on the playground for a few minutes, and I'll meet you there when I'm finished." They hurried to gather their things in their backpacks and headed for the door. "Thank you," Helen said, "and stay together. I won't be long." She added the last, hoping to make it clear to Ms. Slocum that whatever this was about, she wasn't willing to give it more than a few minutes.

"Okay, I'm listening," Helen said when Ms. Slocum hesitated. As the woman moved close enough to speak in a hushed voice, Helen felt her wariness increase.

"I understand you'll be getting married soon."

"That's right."

"Well, perhaps it's none of my business but . . ."

You got that right, Helen responded silently.

"But, you see," Ms. Slocum took on the appearance of an old tortoise, "it's no secret that he didn't treat his first wife well at all, and once she left, the children were in less than favorable circumstances, left alone for hours on end, and—"

"And where exactly did you get this information, Ms. Slocum?" Helen asked, not bothering to keep her tone of voice from expressing her anger.

"That is irrelevant," she insisted. "What is relevant is that—"

"If your information is incorrect, it most certainly is irrelevant. All of this is irrelevant. I'm not going to stand here and listen to you repeat idle gossip just for the sake of it."

"You'd do well to listen to what I have to say if you want to save yourself from a whole lot of misery. Gossip or no, you can't deny the facts that are staring you in the face."

"And what facts would those be?" Helen asked, just wanting Ms. Slocum to trip herself up and illustrate how ridiculous all of this was.

"Well, the neglect of the children, for one. Anyone in their right mind would have turned him in to Social Services at the first sign of—"

"Ms. Slocum," Helen interrupted, knowing that she was implying wrongdoing, "a temporary difficulty with an unreliable baby-sitter is not child neglect. Shayne Brynner is a good man."

"Oh, I'm certain he appears that way. Men always put on their best when they're wanting a woman to marry them. Why, my sister's husband was perfect in every way until he got that ring on her finger. Through the years he became more and more abusive; subtle things, you know. Things that can drive a woman crazy."

Helen sighed, marveling at the ridiculousness of this. "The children love their father. If he was—"

"Miss Starkey," she interrupted, "anyone in their right mind knows that children always tend to cling to the abusive parent, wanting desperately to get their love and validation. You don't know what goes on when you're not around, and you don't know what happened before you came along. I don't like to be the bearer of bad tidings, but . . ."

Oh, but you do, Helen thought. *You love to be the bearer of bad tidings, even if you have to make it up.*

"But you've got to listen to reason, before it's too late. You don't know the truth of what likely happened in that marriage."

"I've spoken with his ex-wife a number of times. She's a selfish and belligerent woman who—"

"And that's just how my sister became after living ten years with a manipulative, abusive—"

"Ms. Slocum," Helen interrupted, raising her hands as she wondered why she had even bothered to get into this. No amount of arguing would ever convince this woman that her greatest motive was simply that misery loves company. She was single, cynical, and unhappy. And so was her sister, obviously. And she apparently didn't want to see Helen join the ranks of married people in this world. She wished that Ms. Slocum could spend some time with Aunt Libby. What a contrast! She took a deep breath and said firmly, "Thank you for your concern. Whatever I am choosing to do with my life is, quite frankly, none of your business. Now, I must go and—"

"I'm only concerned for you, Helen," she said, her voice changing as she took hold of Helen's hand. "I just want you to be happy."

Yeah, right, Helen thought with sarcasm. She resented the intrusion all the more as it became evident Ms. Slocum was justifying her malice and gossip with the belief that she was somehow saving Helen's soul.

"I will be, I can assure you," Helen said and picked up her bag from the desk. "Now, if you will excuse me. The children are waiting."

Ms. Slocum made a noise of disgust as Helen headed toward the door. "Don't say I didn't warn you," she added, as if Helen would be traveling to some third-world country where she might get some dreadful disease from drinking the water.

The bright sunshine and comfortable air hinted at the coming of spring and pushed Ms. Slocum's absurdities quickly out of Helen's mind. The children grabbed their backpacks and came running when they saw her.

Helen hardly thought about Ms. Slocum's "warnings" through the remainder of the day, but as she lay in bed that night, her words began to force their way into Helen's mind. At first she just tried to push them away and disregard them as an absurdity, but then she found herself asking the question: *Could there be some truth to it?* She *had* only assumed that everything Shayne had told her of his relationship with his wife was true. Could it be possible that Margie's leaving was the result of her being treated badly? Did Shayne Brynner behave differently with his children around her than he might privately? As the questions began to gain momentum, Helen sat bolt upright in bed and scolded herself aloud for entertaining such nonsense. She turned on the lamp and read from the Book of Mormon, then prayed for peace enough to sleep. The following day she kept busy enough to prevent the negative thoughts from plaguing her, but they didn't go away.

That evening when Shayne came over to her house for dinner, she felt as glad as ever to see him, but she couldn't suppress the nagging question: *Is he what he seems to be?* She quietly studied her instincts at the dinner table while he chattered with the children about the day's events. None of her instincts gave her reason to believe that Shayne was putting on an act to convince her that he was something different than what he appeared to be. He'd always seemed so genuine and sincere. Or was she simply naive?

Helen considered discussing her feelings with him, just as he'd done when Margie had said hurtful things to him. But what would she say? *Tell me, Mr. Brynner, are you what you appear to be? Or are you really a manipulative jerk in disguise?*

"Are you okay?" Shayne asked, startling her from her thoughts.

"Just a long day," she said, forcing a smile. "How about you?"

"Oh, I'm fine," he said. "Just really tired, for some reason. I must have worked harder than I thought."

"Well, why don't you help the kids finish up their homework and read with them while I clean up here."

Helen was glad for the time alone in the kitchen as she contemplated her dilemma. She uttered a silent prayer as she worked, wanting to feel the peace and happiness she had felt prior to Ms. Slocum's intrusion. When she was finished and went to the family room, she found that the children had gone off to play, and Shayne had kicked off his shoes and was lying on the couch, looking fairly miserable.

"Are you all right?" she asked.

"I don't think so," he said. "It just hit me all of a sudden. I mean . . . I've felt a little under the weather today. But just about the time I sat down I started to ache, and now . . . I'm freezing."

Helen checked his face for fever and found it alarmingly warm. "Good heavens," she said. "I hope it's not that really nasty flu that's going around."

"Me too," he said as Helen covered him with the afghan that had been thrown over the back of the couch. "But whatever it is, it had better be long gone before the first day of spring." He managed a feeble smile. "I've got important plans."

"Right now you'd better just take it easy. At least it's the weekend." A moment later he sat up, and she added, "What are you doing?"

"I'd better go home before it gets any worse."

"You're not driving in this condition."

"Okay," he conceded far too easily. "You can drive me home . . . before it gets any worse."

"No," she concluded, helping him to his feet. "You're staying here where I can take care of you."

"Where are we going?" he asked.

"I'm putting you to bed."

"What bed?"

"My bed," she said, guiding him down the hall. "I'll take the sleeper sofa for as long as I need to. I'll run over to the apartment and get some things for you and the children. But I'm not leaving you to take care of yourself."

"You are so good to me," he said as she threw back the covers and urged him into the bed. Their eyes met as she tucked him in. "I don't know what I ever did to deserve someone as good and beautiful as you."

His sincerity prompted a warm tingle—until it was halted by the memory of Ms. Slocum's accusations against him. Inwardly she cursed the woman for meddling where she didn't belong. She considered calling Carla and talking it through to help her get some perspective, but that wouldn't be easy with Shayne and the children here.

Helen forced her negative thoughts away and concentrated on taking care of Shayne. She gave him some Tylenol and made a list of what he needed from home, then she took the children with her to the apartment to pack bags for themselves and their father. They stopped at the grocery store and stocked up for the weekend, including the makings for homemade chicken noodle soup.

Through the night, Helen checked on Shayne several times and found his fever persisting in spite of the Tylenol, and his body aches were horrible. He insisted that she needed to get her sleep, but her concern for him didn't allow her much rest. The following morning he wasn't hurting as badly, but he felt awful and mostly slept through the day. Helen took a nap in the afternoon while the children watched a video. She woke up feeling more rested, and found Shayne sleeping soundly. Touching his brow, his skin felt slightly warm, but not nearly as feverish as it had been through the night. For a long moment she just watched him, marveling at the love she felt for him and how dramatically he had changed her life. She thought of the bright future they would have together, beginning with a temple marriage. She felt warmth and peace filter through her—then those dreaded doubts crept in, nagging her to believe that this was nothing more than a temporary dream from which she would awaken and find herself confronted with a harsh reality.

Instinctively Helen sat on the edge of the bed, taking hold of Shayne's hand as she closed her eyes and prayed silently for the guidance she needed in order to feel at peace. Through her thoughts she told her Father in Heaven that she considered herself a sound, intelligent woman; she had used every facet of logic to conclude that Shayne Brynner was a good man; and she believed that marrying him was the right thing. She pleaded to know if there was any reason that she should be concerned for herself or the children. Then she felt Shayne squeeze her hand, and she opened her eyes.

"Are you all right?" he asked.

"Of course," she said. "I'm worried about you."

"Oh, I'll be fine," he insisted, "as long as I have you to take care of me. No one's taken care of me during an illness since I left home to go to college."

Helen touched his face, wondering why Margie couldn't have realized what a good man she had. "You rest," she said. "I'm going to make some chicken soup. If your stomach's not bothering you, you can have some later."

"Oh, my stomach's fine," he said. "And *your* chicken soup could definitely bring back my appetite."

While Helen worked in the kitchen, she pondered her feelings and reiterated her prayer. When the soup was finally finished, she fixed a tray for Shayne with a bowl of soup, some crackers, and some red Jell-O. As she entered the bedroom to find him glancing through a magazine, looking pale and exhausted, she stopped in the doorway, suddenly overcome with a sensation somewhere between her heart and her head. The moment she paused, the words appeared in her mind: *He's a good man.* Helen sighed and blinked back her tears as the Spirit confirmed what she had known in her heart all along. Shayne Brynner *was* a good man. And no matter what struggles and difficulties they might face through the course of their lives, she knew they would get through it together.

"Well, hello," he said, glancing up to see her. "Something smells wonderful."

Helen took a deep breath and moved to his side, setting the tray over his lap. "You're hungry. That's a good sign." She touched his face. "No fever. Maybe it was just one of those twenty-four-hour things."

"It certainly had a whop to it, whatever it was. I just hope you and the children don't get it."

"Well, if we do, I know you'll take very good care of us."

"Yes, I will," he said, touching her face in return. "Thank you, Helen."

"For what?"

"For taking care of me. For loving me—and my children. For restoring my faith in love and commitment. And just for being you. I love you just the way you are. I don't want you to ever change. I never believed I could be this happy."

"Well, the feeling is mutual—all of it. And I have to admit that while I certainly don't like your being sick, it's so nice to have you here, and to be able to take care of you. I was happy before I met you, you know. But you and the children have made me happier than I could have ever imagined."

"We're just going to keep getting happier, you know," he said.

"Yes," she smiled and kissed his brow, "I believe we are."

Shayne felt weak and exhausted on Sunday, but by Monday he felt good enough to return to work. Through the week, Helen had the children help her make several batches of lemon bread that were sliced and put into the freezer to be served at the wedding reception. Neither she nor the children got the brief illness that had afflicted Shayne, and they were all grateful. With so much to do, it would have been a definite setback. Helen's mother came a few days before the wedding to help with the final preparations. Everything became a whirlwind as their anticipation of the big event mingled with "to do" lists that just seemed to get longer. Libby came the day before the wedding, and with her arrival the final stages of preparation just seemed to sail smoothly into place.

"You know," she said to Helen the first moment they were alone, "I can't tell you how deeply I was hoping it would come to this. I'd had serious doubts for quite some time that Margie would commit herself to making that marriage work, and when I met you, I just felt in my heart that you could be the one to make Shayne happy. He's a good man, and he deserves a woman as good as you."

Helen smiled with tears in her eyes and embraced Libby firmly. "Thank you," she said. "You can't know what that means to me." She laughed softly and they took each other's hands. "And I can't tell you how thrilled I am to know that you're going to be my aunt, too. Everybody ought to have an Aunt Libby."

"You're too sweet," Libby said, and they hugged again.

That evening, Helen tried on her dress one last time to make certain everything was in order. Libby and her mother made such a fuss that Helen couldn't help giggling like a child. Taking in her appearance now, she had to admit that the dress was every bit as flattering as she'd hoped. It disguised her figure flaws well, and actually made her look like she had a waistline. She had to admit that she'd never felt more beautiful, but she knew the reality of that feeling was in seeing herself through Shayne's eyes. And the following morning, when she finally emerged from the bride's room of the temple, she felt almost like an angel, floating on some ethereal cloud of happiness. When Shayne saw her, the message in his eyes didn't disappoint her. His love truly made her feel more beautiful than she ever had in her life.

All of their preparations paid off as the day of the wedding moved along perfectly. Carla proved herself the truest of friends as she spent every minute on her feet, seeing that the reception came together without a glitch. It had been Carla's idea to hang yards of shimmery gold fabric in strips down the walls and from the ceiling, with rows of tiny white lights dangling against them, giving the illusion of stars twinkling all around the room. The effect was intensified by hundreds of little cardboard stars, cut in different sizes by third-graders and spray-painted gold, hanging from the ceiling with fishing line. Scotty and Tamara served as best man and maid of honor, and nearly every one of Helen's students came to the reception with their parents. For Helen, the only thing that made the entire day less than perfect was the absence of Shayne's parents, who were still serving their mission in South America. But they had called the day before, and Helen had met them over the phone. She was touched by their warm wishes, and looked forward to the day when they would return.

When the reception was finally coming to a close and it was time to cut the cake, Helen felt momentarily detached from herself, as if she were in a dream and somehow observing this from a distance. She loved Shayne more than she could possibly express, just as she loved his children. And standing with him amidst this profusion of stars, with the memories of a temple marriage still tingling through her, it was easy to imagine being together forever. But it wasn't a dream, she reminded herself. It was real. It was life. And she would live it to its fullest.

LEMON BREAD

> *1 lemon cake mix*
> *1 3 oz. instant lemon pudding*
> *1/3 cup oil*
> *2 eggs*
> *1 cup water*

Mix ingredients and pour into 2 well-greased loaf pans.
Bake at 350° for 35 to 40 minutes.
Cool in pan, then top with glaze.

Glaze:
> *1/2 cup powdered sugar*
> *4 tablespoons lemon juice*

Epilogue

Seven Months Later

Scotty and Tamara pressed their faces against the glass of the huge airport window, watching the jetliner taxi toward the gate. Helen felt Shayne squeeze her hand, and she sensed his excitement at seeing his parents again. All of his family members, including Libby, were here, just as they had been at the wedding. The children—more than twenty of them—bubbled with the same anticipation the adults were feeling. But Helen knew that for Shayne it was more intense than for his siblings. When his parents had left on their mission eighteen months earlier, he had been married to someone else, and they'd had no reason to believe that their son's marriage had more than the usual challenges. Through letters, he had been able to convey all that had happened and the emotions involved for all of them. Their correspondence, in return, had expressed their concern over his divorce, as well as their joy at his finding a new wife. And his parents had been pleased with the news that they were now expecting a baby—although Helen doubted that anyone could be more happy about that than she was. But she had yet to meet her new in-laws face to face, and she couldn't deny the irony in the situation.

As Shayne's parents came through the gate, Helen easily recognized them from their pictures. And they each bore a resemblance to Shayne that she found endearing. She stood back with Shayne, her hand in his, until they had greeted every other member of the family, including Scotty and Tamara. When they finally came face to face, nothing was said before they each gave Shayne a hearty embrace. Then his mother turned to Helen. As their eyes met, Helen expected an amiable greeting, perhaps even a hug. But Suzanne Brynner took Helen's hands into hers at the same moment tears appeared in her eyes. In a voice soft enough that only Helen could hear, she said, "Thank you, Helen. Thank you for being there for him when we couldn't be. Deep in my heart, I've known for a long time that the situation wasn't good, and I worried so much. When we left on our mission, I knew I couldn't be consumed with worry for my children, and I asked the Lord to send a guiding star for my son to get him through." She embraced Helen tightly and murmured close to her ear, "You have no idea how literally you have been the answer to many prayers, my dear. And I thank the Lord that you're the kind of woman who is capable of doing just that."

Suzanne drew back, and Helen's focus was blurred by the mist in her eyes. But she had to admit, "All I did was fall in love with his children—and then him, of course. It is I who should be thanking you . . . for raising such a fine man. I never dreamed I could be this happy."

"As you deserve to be," Suzanne said. Then her husband took hold of Helen and gave her a fatherly embrace, as if he had done so a thousand times before.

"Welcome to the family, Mrs. Brynner," he said, and Helen couldn't help but love him immediately. "I've been counting the minutes until I could meet you. And we're so thrilled about the baby. We can't have too many of those." He gave a deep laugh, and Helen laughed with him.

"No, I don't suppose we can," Helen said.

"Will you keep teaching?" he asked.

"Of course," she said. "The school is wonderful about working with such things, and Shayne's more than willing to help out."

"He got that from me." He laughed again, and Helen tenderly imagined Shayne at this age. It was evident he had much in common with his father. There was so much she wanted to say, but she was suddenly overcome with so much emotion that she didn't dare speak. She felt Shayne's arm come around her just as Scotty and Tamara moved into their little circle, full of excitement at being with their grandparents again.

"You know," Shayne whispered in Helen's ear, as if he'd read her mind, "life just doesn't get any better than this."

Helen looked up at him and tried to blink back the tears, but she knew he saw them. "No, it doesn't," she murmured. *If only Ms. Slocum could see me now,* she thought, and smiled as the family moved together to the luggage claim before they would all go to a restaurant for lunch. Life just didn't get any better than this.

ABOUT THE AUTHOR

Anita Stansfield has been writing for more than twenty years, and her best-selling novels have captivated and moved hundreds of thousands of readers with their deeply romantic stories and focus on important contemporary issues. Her interest in creating romantic fiction began in high school, and her work has appeared in national publications. *A Star in Winter* is her sixteenth novel to be published by Covenant.

Anita lives with her husband, Vince, and their five children and two cats in Alpine, Utah.

Acknowledgments

In sharing some of my favorite recipes with you, it's only appropriate that I give credit where credit is due. Recipes are like uplifting thoughts. They get passed around and some become well known, while many of us have no idea where they originated or who deserves the credit. Many of these recipes were passed down from my mother, and making them brings her to mind. I believe food is one of many ways a legacy is passed through the generations. Her recipes include the Porcupine Meatballs, Coffee Cake, and Fruitcake. The Hamburger Pie recipe is from my neighbor Deann, in Springville, who was always an inspiration in the kitchen. I got the Meat Loaf recipe in a high school cooking class. (It was my idea to cook it in a ring.) The Lemon Bread came from someone sharing it at Relief Society. The Chicken Enchiladas came from my neighbor, Shellie, who brought them over after my last baby was born. And the others, I came up with on my own. Writing generally supersedes my desire to be in the kitchen. But hey, we've got to eat. Enjoy!!

AN EXCERPT FROM THE LONG-AWAITED SEQUEL TO
SECRETS OF THE HEART, A NOVEL BY JOANN JOLLEY

PROLOGUE

"You're thinking about him, aren't you?"

Paula Donroe winced as her son's deep voice pulled her back to the present. "Hmm? I suppose," she murmured, setting the bulky Sunbeam® iron on its heel. It teetered for a second at one end of the long, fabric-covered ironing board, then settled into a statue-like stillness.

"Figures," Scott muttered as he slouched against the door frame of his mother's bedroom.

Paula took a deep breath before turning to face her tall, sullen, sixteen-year-old son. *Easy does it,* she silently cautioned herself. *We've all been through an emotional wringer lately, and he's probably hurting just as much as the rest of us. Maybe more . . . he was there when the shot was fired, after all.* An achingly familiar surge of grief rippled through her chest at the thought, and a moment later she felt an empathetic smile rise to her lips. "What do you mean, sweetie?"

"Nuthin'. It's all you ever think about." He stretched out one leg, dug the heel of his sneaker into the carpet, and dragged his foot slowly backward to make a long, wide furrow in the deep pile.

"Well, Scotty," she said, moving close enough to see the sparse patches of adolescent stubble on his chin, "it's only been a few weeks. We all need a little time, don't you think?" She reached out to touch his shoulder and felt the lean, hard muscles tense beneath his over-sized yellow T-shirt.

"Yeah." He set his jaw in a rigid line and stared at the floor.

"You know, honey," she ventured, "if you'd like to talk about it, we could always—"

"Nuthin' to talk about." He shrugged away her hand and smoothed the carpet with a circular motion of his foot. "I gotta go."

Paula sighed. *Maybe next week . . . next month . . . next year.* "Okay. Mind if I ask where you're off to so early on a Saturday morning?" She steeled herself for the all-too-familiar response.

"The clubhouse."

"I see." Her voice was deliberately pleasant, even though she wanted to lash out at him, tell him he should find better things to do with his life than spend every waking moment with that useless gang of his. *But you can't risk driving him even further away,* she reminded herself. *Just love him and be patient—remember the eternal perspective. Let him know you care, and eventually he might return the favor.* "And how are the Crawlers doing these days?"

"Cool."

"That's nice, dear." *Patience—that's the key. Perhaps one day he'll actually speak to you in sentences of more than three words.* "Try to be home at a reasonable hour, will you?"

"Right," he growled, disappearing quickly into the hall. A few seconds later, she heard the front door slam.

Shaking her head, Paula turned back to the ironing board. She carefully smoothed the crinkled front panel of a pale-blue oxford shirt, dampened it with a spray bottle, and lowered the iron to the fabric. A slow hissing sound accompanied a few light bursts of steam as the rumpled cotton cloth yielded to the hot metal and tightened, then relaxed into a polished, wrinkle-free surface.

For some unexplained reason, this simple act of ironing had, over the last month or so, become a comfortable and comforting routine for Paula. She had moved the ironing board upstairs to her bedroom, where she now stood facing the open window overlooking the front yard of her suburban home in Woodland Hills, California. In this peaceful setting, she would sometimes spend hours banishing the wrinkles from a large assortment of shirts, blouses, and slacks. Her favorite was 100% cotton. None of the permanent-press garments would rumple enough to give her the satisfaction of restoring their original crispness. But cotton—there was a fabric she could really work with. Its wrinkles were so deep and defined that by the time she had sprayed and ironed and smoothed and creased, she was in absolute control. Maybe that was it—the sense of control. It was what she needed most in her life at the moment. If she couldn't quite get the wrinkles in her mind and heart straightened out, at least she could take care of the wrinkles in her laundry.

On this Saturday morning in mid-January, Paula now returned to the thoughts that had absorbed her before Scott's interruption. Yes, she'd been thinking about him—about *both* of them. Her mind roamed over the details of her life since that bleak day in early November when her world had changed forever. TJ, her bright, funny, basketball-crazy twelve-year-old son, had been shot in a random act of violence as he and Scott and some friends had cruised the streets of downtown Los Angeles. He had lived less than a day; and in many ways Paula had felt that his senseless death was her fault. They had argued that morning because he wanted to join the Mormon Church. Paula had flatly refused to give her permission, and TJ, in his frustration, had taken off with Scott. Hours later, the final moments of his life had played themselves out in a cold, indifferent hospital room.

But it hasn't been all bad, Paula reminded herself as she nudged the tip of the iron into a v-shaped pleat on the back of the shirt. *There have been miracles, too.* She smiled, relaxing a little as the warmer memories took hold. After TJ's death, the Mormon missionaries, Elders Richland and Stucki, had taught her the gospel, and she had finally come to understand why her young son had been so determined to join the Church: it was *true*. On a golden morning just before Thanksgiving, she and Millie, her housekeeper and friend, had been baptized. TJ had been there, too, dressed in white, a joyful grin illuminating his freckled face. Paula had seen him.

As quickly as it had come, her expression of gratitude was submerged in a wave of doubt, even despair. *But where is he now?* she questioned silently. She knew where he was, of course—home on a farm just outside Roberts, Idaho, where he'd been since the first of December, the final day of his mission. They had stood together in the Los Angeles airport saying their good-byes, she knowing the marvelous secret of his parentage, wondering when and how she would ever be able to tell him. Then, placing his lips close to her ear, he had whispered that *he knew.* He had seen the look in her eyes that Thanksgiving Day, had discerned the meaning in her subtle questions about his family, and now confirmed the joyful truth at their moment of parting. When she'd caught her breath, they had embraced, wept, promised to stay in touch. Knowing he was on his way to a long-awaited family reunion, she would stand back and let him make the first contact. "Call . . . write . . . whatever," she had whispered. "Whenever you're ready. I'll be waiting."

"I will," he had promised.

Paula's brow furrowed, and the iron stopped its rhythmic back-and-forth motion. *That was six weeks ago,* she mused. *Christmas, New Year's . . . times I would have expected a call, or at least a card. What's going on?* She plunged deeper into thought, considering all the troubling possibilities. *Is he ill? Has he decided he doesn't want me in his life after all? Has he told his parents, and have they forbidden him to contact me? Do I mean anything at all to him, or am I just another notch on his missionary name tag? Will I ever see or hear—*

"Ow-w-w!" Paula smelled the seared flesh on one side of her finger almost at the same instant she felt the white-hot pain. "Nice move, Donroe," she sputtered as a fiery red welt erupted and spread itself alongside her knuckle. "What were you thinking? That's your problem, you know—you were thinking *too much.*" Her reflexes took over, and she raised the finger to her lips and sucked hard. With her other hand, she yanked on the iron's garish blue cord until the socket gave up and let go. Lifting the iron, she saw an angry brown scorch mark on the shirt's pale-blue sleeve. "So much for being in control," she muttered.

With her throbbing finger still pressed to her lips, she set the iron on its heel and moved a few steps to her bed. Sinking onto the polished-cotton comforter, she began to rock back and forth, her eyes closed tightly in an effort to shut out the pain. *Get a grip, girl,* she chided. *It's only a little burn.* But somehow this minor insult to her flesh was the last straw, and a suffocating wave of grief and helplessness washed over her. Hot tears coursed down her cheeks as she thought of her three sons—TJ, who now lay beneath a mound of cold earth in the Rolling Hills Cemetery; Scott, who seemed to be moving further away from her by the minute; and Mark Richland, the precious child she had found but now seemed to have lost again. "What's it all for, Heavenly Father?" she sobbed. "What's it all for?"

Falling back against the pillows, Paula yielded to the emotion of the moment. She wept until exhaustion stilled her slender body and she fell into a heavy, dreamless sleep.

Sydney

0   1 km

0   1 mile

Port Jackson

Garden
Island

Clarke
Island

Point
Piper

Woollahra
Point

Darling Point

POTTS
POINT

*Elizabeth
Bay*

*Elizabeth
Point*

*Rose
Bay*

*Elizabeth
Bay House*

5

ELIZABETH
BAY

*Double
Bay*

South   Head   Road

*El Alamein
Fountain*

*Rushcutters
Bay*

DOUBLE
BAY

South

Victoria

S CROSS

RUSHCUTTERS
BAY PARK

RUSHCUTTERS
BAY

Road

Road

Bayswater Rd

Head

Bellevue

St

Neild

Avenue

South

Head

Road

Road

Glenmore

Road

TRUMPER
PARK

Ocean

Edgecliff Road

ford

PADDINGTON

EDGECLIFF

COOPER   PARK

*Victoria
Barracks*

Street

Jersey

Street

Road

OORE

Moore

Park

Road

Edgecliff

Road

PARK

Oxford   Street

Sydney

Einfeld

Drive

Oxford

Street

Road

BONDI

Bronte

Ebley St

York

Birrell

Street

CENTENNIAL
PARK

JUNCTION

Anzac

Parade

Alison Street

Tours